ELEVATOR INCIDENT OF 2016

Saana Lahtinen

ELEVATOR INCIDENT OF 2016

© 2025 Saana Lahtinen

Publisher: BoD · Books on Demand, Mannerheimintie 12 B,
00100 Helsinki, bod@bod.fi
Print: Libri Plureos GmbH, Friedensallee 273, 22763
Hamburg, Germany
ISBN: 978-952-80-8252-1

To the most precious being in this universe, Dara.

ENTERTAINMENT!!

I wanted to stay awake longer. The day had been horrible, like pushing a rock up a never-ending hill, and a craving for something nice was overwhelming. A small thing, like a funny joke that would at least make me smile or laugh, *weakly*. However, that tiny thing felt impossible to ask for. It was January, early January, which is not as bad as *late* January. The excitement of the new year was still in the air, but soon enough it would be overshadowed by the bleakness of winter. It was snowing heavily, and I sat on the couch with my dog. She was a schipperke with more fur than a so-called normal one. Her fur was dark and in the middle of the night, she blended into the shadows with her small body. Only her eyes glowed, revealing the dog's position.

The TV was on; I was hoping that in between the advertisements for mostly useless things something funny would appear and make me laugh. No, it felt like laughter was too much to ask from the universe, a simple smile would be enough for me to call it a night. Soon, a possible distraction from reality appeared on the screen. A pig wearing a suit, sitting like a human, and smiling oddly caught my attention.

"Ladies and gentlemen, welcome!" The pig said with a strong scratchy voice. It sounded as if the animal was a chain smoker. *"Today we have a guest! The one and only Mr. Brown!"*

Clapping and cheering erupted as the cameras turned to face the audience full of animals: giraffes, armadillos, elephants, flamingos, dogs, cats, peacocks, etc. Then, Mr. Brown, a brown bear, walked to the stage, waving his paw, and greeting the suit-wearing pig. My dog noticed the absurdity of the show and focused on the screen. Her ears were pointed up and her eyes followed the animals' movements.

"Great to have you here, Mr. Brown. Looks like you're the fan-favorite!"

"Wow, that's wonderful to hear. Thank you so much for having me as a guest. This is a dream come true for me." The bear said, breathy.

"Lovely!" The pig smiled. *"Well, I need to ask the question."*

"Go ahead, I think the audience is dying to know."

"How do you manage this newfound fame? You jumped from being an unknown actor to the most known actor almost overnight! Your performance has gained many nominations for awards." The pig spoke fast and loudly, alternating between speaking to Mr. Brown and the audience.

"It's a lot, I'll admit it, but it's so worth it. Never would I've dreamed of this; auditioning for fun changed my life. I didn't have any prior experience and didn't think I had any chance, but here I am! It feels wonderful and I just want to thank everyone."

"Oh, that's right! Your first role is your breakthrough role, congratulations!"

"Thank you, I got really lucky." Mr. Brown replied.

"Do you have anything to say to aspiring actors?" The pig motioned for the camera to zoom in on the bear's face.

"Don't limit yourself by focusing too much on the outcome. You'll lose opportunities and enjoyment if you don't let things flow."

I stared at the screen, bewildered that Mr. Brown's words struck something in my heart. The show seemed like a fever dream, and I shook my head to wake myself up to find out that I wasn't asleep. I reached for the remote, but my dog's paw landed on it before my hand did. I stared at the dog, amused. My smile dropped as she bared her teeth. The dog's brown eyes held such intensity that the message was clear; let her watch the show.

CATCHING ALLURE

From the moment the airplane took off to its landing, there had been continuous arguing between Juno and Santiago. Not even the warmth of the Spanish sun could calm the two down, especially Juno. The group stood in silence, listening to them bickering about which way was fastest to the small village where they'd spend an entire week, celebrating graduating from university. Santiago, who was from Spain, knew the best route because he had visited the village before. Juno, an American woman, who had never been to Spain, insisted she knew better. Penelope, Aloisio, and Helene stared at the two arguing, refusing to step in. Anyone who had conversed with Juno knew how she was; her way or nothing. Discussing anything with that woman was an exhausting battle you couldn't win.

"Can we just go get the car?" Aloisio interrupted the two, tired of their endless fighting. He was beginning to regret accepting the invite from Helene to join the trip. He could've stayed in London and spent this time with his closest friends instead of listening to Juno and Santiago, of all people. "You two have plenty of time to disagree in the car."

"I'm driving," Santiago hissed. "And *I'm* the one who decides the route." He stomped off to the rental office inside the airport. Juno started ranting, saying she knew better. She could read a map, *unlike Santiago*. Helene tried to argue with her, saying that he had been there before, but her defenses fell on deaf ears. Aloisio felt his head beginning to hurt out of frustration, wondering if he still could flee this situation, and book a flight back home. His cat, *Gato*, stayed back home with a friend. Aloisio began to miss the company of his grumpy cat.

It didn't take long for Santiago to get the keys to the rental car. With a thick silence, the group looked for the car in the parking lot in the relentless heat. In whispers, Santiago begged others to sit in the passenger seat instead of Juno, yet he was unsuccessful. Penelope sat in the middle since she was the shortest, Aloisio on her right side, and Helene on her left. It was early afternoon until the group managed to start their three-hour drive to the countryside village. Aloisio tried to sleep, but Juno's passive-aggressive remarks and Helene's flirting with Santiago made it impossible. Penelope kept silent for the most part, yet when she spoke it was only agreement never disagreement.

The village was smaller than Aloisio thought. Beautiful, perhaps stuck in time, and calm. On the outskirts of the village, he noticed an old church. It was made of stone and the building blended into the dry nature around it. Most churches look out of place for him and this one was no exception, yet it was more bothersome than usual. In his eyes, the building slowly moved toward him, or he was moving toward it.

"What're you looking at?" Helene asked.

"Just a church," he pointed at it. "There, in the distance."

"Wow, historic. Bet you'll like that."

"Why do you think that?" He asked, confused.

"Why wouldn't you? Didn't you major in history?"

"No, I did classics." He replied, even more confused.

"Oh."

Helene and Aloisio weren't close by any means, but they'd known each other for almost two years. He didn't expect her to know every single detail about him, yet he knew the basics about Helene. She studied biology and she was from Manchester. He was slightly hurt that a person he considered somehow a friend didn't have the decency to remember anything about him, but it wasn't surprising since the only person she cared about was Santiago. Aloisio couldn't blame Helene since he also *cared* about him. Their shared interest was mostly because of his looks, not his personality. Santiago could be an asshole.

The villa rented by Santiago was big: everyone had their own room, three bathrooms, a big kitchen, and a living room. Penelope was most excited about the pool. Juno took the biggest room which led to arguing between Helene and her, but it was decided by Juno that she deserved it more. Helene calmed down after Santiago chose the room beside hers.

"Oh, gosh. I don't know which room I want." Penelope wondered. Aloisio stayed quiet, waiting for her to choose. "What room would you take if you were me?"

"I don't know," he replied. "I'm not you."

"Just think for a second that you were me." She insisted.

"The one further from the front door, I guess." He didn't try to think like her, he just wanted to get this over with.

"I don't know." She murmured. It was always like this with Penelope; she can't make decisions by herself. Basic, everyday situations get her stuck, and others have to pull her out of it.

"If you don't know, can I just take the room near the front door?" Aloisio sighed, irritated by her lack of decisiveness.

"I guess that's fine…"

"Do you want the room by the front door?" He heard the disappointment in her tone. Penelope shrugged her shoulders and continued to stare at the hallway with the rooms, waiting for their guests. "You can take the room if you want it, Penelope."

"I can't decide–"

"I insist you take the room." He said, firmly. Penelope walked over to the door, glancing back at Aloisio from time to time. When she entered the room, he rolled his eyes.

The room was spacious with a view of the damn church. His gaze always landed on the building whether he wanted to or not. It didn't take long for Santiago to barge into his room, talking about the women of Spain and how he was going to get lucky this week.

"We are hitting the club tonight–"

"Is there a club?" Aloisio asked. "Seriously, this place is tiny as shit."

"There has to be!" Santiago exclaimed.

"Uh-huh, well, what if there isn't?" He proposed.

"We'll just buy booze and drink, duh. We have a pool and this big-*ass* villa."

Aloisios' suspicion was correct; the village didn't have a club. The few markets it had were small and options limited.

"I swear to God you jinxed it." Santiago huffed, carrying the bags of alcohol.

"Sure, blame me all you want," Aloisio said, lighting his cigarette.

It didn't take long for Helene to get drunk. She was always a lightweight. She laid on a sunchair, holding a glass of tequila mixed with soda. She giggled at every word that left Santiago's mouth. Aloisio didn't pay attention to what the rest were doing, he kept staring at the church in the distance. The sunset made the building a haunting sight, yet mesmerizing.

"What are you looking at?" Juno asked.

"The church." He responded, not taking his eyes off it.

"What church?"

"That one," he pointed at it. In his eyes, the building began to sway from side to side, almost calling him toward it.

"Ew," Juno grimaced. "Looks weird." Aloisio hummed in agreement, wanting to stop looking at it, yet being unable to do so. "We should check it out."

"What?" He asked, bewildered.

"We should check the church out," Juno repeated.

"I don't think that's a good idea–"

"Why the hell not?" She inquired, annoyed that someone disagreed with her.

"I didn't see a church inside this village," Aloisio thought. "So, that one must still be in use. I think– I think it should be left alone."

"Santiago!" Juno yelled. "You see that church?"

"Yeah, what about it?" He asked.

"Let's check it out." She said.

"Why would I want to check out a church? I don't give a fuck."

"Yeah, who gives a fuck–" Helene slurred, giggling.

"Fine, I'll go there by myself." Juno stood up, put her skirt, and sandals back on.

"Should you go there alone?" Penelope asked, timid.

"Oh, please, I can handle it," Juno hissed. "It's a goddamn church and ya'll are just a bunch of pussies." Santiago felt challenged and rose to his feet, tequila bottle in hand. *His ego would be the death of him*, Aloisio thought. "Why don't we all go?" Helene proposed, smiling like an idiot. Penelope looked hesitant, frightened even, yet everybody knew she wouldn't fight back. Just with one statement Juno managed to get everyone else on her side.

"You're coming too, Aloisio," Santiago ordered.

"Fine, whatever." He sighed. The church bothered him, but he didn't have to go inside, he could just stay outside and let the others act like idiots.

The sun had set, leaving only faint lights illuminating the otherwise dark countryside. Juno and Santiago had their phone flashlights on, leading the rest toward the old building. Aloisio trailed behind, slowly. The church was calling him, yet his gut told him to stay away. The others, mainly the pair always arguing, dove into things without thinking. He wondered if they possessed any survival instincts. They never knew when to back down. Penelope, on the other hand, lacked any defense skills. She only followed others. Helene, a codependent personality, who latched onto others, ignoring her own personal needs lacked assertiveness like Penelope. He felt like walking among sheep, but he could only blame himself since he chose to follow the rest. He wasn't any better; maybe he was just a judgemental piece of shit and nothing else.

The church was bigger than he anticipated, and it left a deep primal fear in him. That's when he decided *he was getting the fuck out of there*. Aloisio turned around and started walking back toward the village with only little lights left.

"Where are you going?" Juno yelled.

"Back to the villa." He replied without turning to face the group.

"Are you that scared?" Santiago laughed.

"Maybe!"

The walk back took longer. He felt like the village had moved further away from the church. It was impossible yet the thought lingered at the back of his mind. The village streets were empty, and every house had gone to sleep. The streetlights flickered and Aloisio felt more uncomfortable with each passing second, he wasn't inside the villa. He reached the rented building, glancing behind him. Clumsily, he opened the door and locked it behind him. Inside his room, he closed the curtains, refusing to take a look at the church in the distance. He laid his head on the soft pillow, sleep overtaking him fast.

The church floated in his dreams. It molded into every unconscious scenario, he only focused on the church and nothing else. A bigger church, a smaller church, the church in his city of origin, the church back in his university apartment, the church in his hands, the church *in his room at the villa,* and the church underwater in the backyard pool.

Aloisio woke up in a panic, forgetting his whereabouts. It didn't take him long to remember where he was. Weak sunlight tried to invade the room through the curtains. He checked his phone: 06:55 in the morning. *He had no signal.* The strange teleporting and morphing church from his dreams was still fresh in his mind until memories from last night started flooding. *Juno, Santiago, Helene, Penelope, where the fuck were they?* The last place he'd seen them was at the church.

They weren't inside the house; their beds were untouched. *Went to get breakfast?* Hell, no. None of them were early birds. *Needed something from the store?* The small stores weren't open this early. *Passed out somewhere outside the village?* Penelope didn't drink, she would've called him for help if the rest had drunk too much.

The sunlight reflected on the water's surface, blinding him. The backyard looked empty: the ashtray he had used was gone, the sun chairs were missing, and no bottles from yesterday were there. It didn't take long to find the items.

The pool was filled with everything. He wondered if the others pulled a sick and twisted prank on him. Aloisio didn't find it funny. He felt his heart drop, almost falling to his stomach. The sudden overwhelming feeling left him nauseous. He ran back inside the house and rummaged through Santiago's room, looking for the car keys. His hands trembled, and cold sweats sent shivers down his spine.

The village was a ghost town; curtains were closed, and no establishments were open. He drove through the village, ignoring speed limits. The church stood tall, taller than yesterday, and he wondered how Penelope, Juno, and Helene had ended up from there to the bottom of the pool. He stepped on the gas, trying to forget the image of his friends' lifeless bodies. The road was made of dirt with dry empty fields everywhere, only the goddamn church occupied it with its disgusting allure. The building invaded the image of the bodies; it was also underwater. It had made its home inside his mind, and it caused his head to ache. Aloisio closed his eyes, fearing a vein might burst in his brain. Against his will, the church became one with him. It would always be there.

The car hit something, throwing the *thing* onto the hood and breaking the windshield. He stopped the car, terrified of what he might've caused. Slowly, with shaking limbs, he exited the vehicle to see what had dropped onto the dirt road. There he lay, gasping for breath with contorted extremities. Santiago tried pleading but he could only wheeze in agony. Aloisio stared at him, emotionless.

"I'm sorry," he whispered to him. "*I'm not* fucking going down because of you. This is all your fault anyway. You could've avoided this if you just had left it alone, I told you all dickheads to leave it." The apology was genuine, but he couldn't control the rest of the words. He felt possessed by a natural force, so old and familiar.

"Was it worth it?" He hissed at the dying man. "You wanted to experience it for yourselves," he ranted, unable to stop. "The eons-old material built to be something else. It's not supposed to be in that form, it was supposed to stay where it pleases. Not go where *you people* wanted."

"This is what you fucking clowns deserve." It looked around, got inside the car, and drove over Santiago. He made noises as his bones cracked, but silence followed quickly. It drove off, leaving the mangled man in the middle of the road.

OVERGROWN TOMATO

A small red hand, reached out from behind our mother's shoulder. His skin was the same shade as a tomato, and he wasn't too much bigger than the vegetable either. His birthday landed on the day before mine. We're almost exactly four years apart. For a long time, it bothered me that I had to share my birthday with my younger brother. Only during the last decade, I've begun to appreciate February, our birth month.

Our birthdays are ordinary days, no longer treated like big celebrations since we're both older. He's no longer the tomato-colored crying baby I saw on my fourth birthday. As we grew, our inherited facial features shaped similarly. He'll always be a younger version of me, and I'll always be an older version of him. Each year, I wait for his birthday. He's no longer small, he's almost the same height as me. My ego wishes he wouldn't grow taller than me, but my heart wants him to grow as tall as a skyscraper.

VIRTUAL KNIGHT

Hues of green, blue, and purple shine in its armor. The knight lacked everything except beauty and prowess. No soul, body, or thoughts, yet it moved on command. *Pure perfection*, a common opinion of anyone who laid eyes on the magnificent creation. The knight held the highest potential. Emotions, desires, or rules wouldn't hold it back.

The creator disagreed. She didn't create to fulfill others' expectations, she created to bring parts of her soul into the physical world. Emotions, desires, and rules were what the knight needed. The sword it carried needed to be roughed up, the weapon's pristine condition strengthened the knight's image of perfection. It needed flesh, it needed to bleed like the creator. The knight had to have emotions and desires to feed its soul.

A good mother would let her child live as they pleased, but not her. She was never cut out for motherhood. She demanded the imperfection of herself. The knight needed to be a version of her, just physically more durable.

The knight grew tired of its creator's constant pressure. The first emotion it felt was melancholy. A wave of hopelessness nestled over the knight. Soon, its thoughts began to form. A desire for acceptance surged. It dreamed of the creator's words of encouragement, love, and pride.

The knight never received what it craved. Soon, it flung the sword, cutting through flesh. She fell, eyes wide open, and caught off guard. The knight felt remorse, it had acted out of rage. The creator was in awe as she stared at her attacker. Lights reflected off the knight, creating a bursting aura of lavender and turquoise around her creation. She saw it, a small flicker of life, sneak its way through the unbreakable armor inside the hollow being.

FEBRUARY 11th–17th, 2024

A good start to the day is in the air, sipping on an overpriced gin and tonic. The flight is full; however, my row is an exception. I'm sitting in the window seat, 19A, which I paid an arm and a leg for. The middle seat is empty, but an older gentleman sits in the aisle seat. We're both Finnish, but against our nature, we struck up a short conversation about our empty middle seat while someone was having a medical emergency a few rows away from us.

The plane landed safely, and I darted out of it, of course, only after the EMTs escorted the man with the medical emergency out of the plane. The airport was packed with people, which unsettled me. It felt harder and harder to breathe the longer I stayed inside, so I almost ran like a maniac to the taxis outside.

In the taxi, I felt relieved. I melted into the hard seats. It was arctic in Finland, and I had many layers on, so sweating started the moment the plane landed. At the accommodation, a gut-wrenching feeling of nostalgia scratched my chest. I wanted to crawl out of my meat suit and be one with the building. It's my second time in this place. I was shown a room that would be mine for the coming week. It's on the fifth floor. The door closes behind me and I feel trapped. I throw my bags down, peel off all the layers like I was an onion, change clothes, and run down the stairs almost tripping on my feet. It's dark outside and rains like hell, but I couldn't care less. My heart beats wildly while the rain pounds on my red umbrella. Everything the umbrella doesn't cover gets soaked.

I don't have to use a map; I know the city like the back of my hand. I let my instincts guide me. They lead me to a restaurant, I sit inside and stare into the streets and all the people running for shelter from the assaulting rain. I downed my drink, paid for it, and rushed into the rain.

…

The night was rough due to my tendency to get extremely anxious. My room has an old heater at the end of my bed, and it's turned on. If you get close to it, you're able to smell dust and smoke. I was convinced that I'd die because of carbon monoxide poisoning, and that my body would rot until someone noticed the smell. I might've only slept for about three hours because I was nauseous and worried about the damn heater killing me in my sleep. A certain ticking noise also occupied my thoughts. It rained almost for the whole night, it was soothing, but it also caused the ticking noise. I listened to it for hours since I couldn't find a way to stop it. I looked through my small room: the window, the heater, the lamps, the closet, under the bed. I even looked and listened to my phone to make sure that it wasn't going to explode and burn me alive. When the rain stopped, so did the ticking sound.

My Portuguese class starts today. I think I was anxious about it, which is strange since I've been to this language school three times before. It's not a new experience for me. Grammar, speaking, grammar, writing, grammar, grammar… That's how it goes.

After my class I had to return to my room to shed some clothes; +20°C and full-blown sunshine were almost overwhelming for me after sitting in the cold darkness of my home country for the last four months. My sunglasses feel out of place on my face since I rarely get to use them. The glasses are like shields, suddenly I believe I'm invincible.

Lisbon is full of uphill and downhill. My legs are used to it, but I can't say the same about my lungs. I dragged myself up to Jardim do Torel, the climb was tough, yet worth it. The views are lovely, I can see every color of the rainbow merge together in all the old buildings next to each other. Someone is playing an instrument in the distance, I don't know what type of instrument it is, and I'll be honest, I don't really care. I wish I could sit on this bench forever, and marvel at these centuries-old buildings all around me. I want to be glued to the bench, but I'd get bored fast, and pull myself free, tearing my skin off.

After leaving the garden, all emotions, smells, and noises around me hit me like a truck. I felt my legs growing weaker and the nausea started up again. I found my way to a restaurant, thinking that a good drink and some food is what I need. The Long Island iced tea I ordered didn't make me feel better. I don't even taste the alcohol in it, I was hoping that getting tipsy would rid me of my nausea. When the pepperoni flatbread came into my view, I knew I had made a big mistake ordering it. It looked good, marvelous even. I wanted to eat the whole thing, but the first bite almost came back up. I promised my mother that I'd eat at least one full meal every day; I'll have to break that promise. The waiter asks me if everything is alright, I couldn't bring myself to tell him the truth, so I just asked for a to-go box. I walk out the door and the sunlight punches me in the face. I feel like I'm okay again.

I don't notice that I've walked closer to my accommodation. I forget that I'm in Lisbon. I don't feel like a real person, I haven't felt like one in almost a decade and I'm only twenty.

Someone stops me, it's a man. He's shorter than me and I stare down at him. That's not my intention, yet I can't help it. I stop to talk to him because I'd feel bad if I didn't listen to him. He wants me to eat at his restaurant, but I tell him that I already ate and point at the to-go box full of pepperoni flatbread that *I won't* eat. He tells me that my Portuguese is good. He wants to know if my fluency is because of a boyfriend. I didn't learn a language for a man, I don't do things for men. I laugh and tell him that I just like the language, that's all. The man asks for my name and without hesitation, I tell him my real name. The man tells me his name and we shake hands, I tell him that it's a pleasure to meet him. I wasn't lying, I was happy for our small conversation. He gives me a card that has information on his restaurant, and I take it to be polite. He calls me beautiful and kind. I know, I know, he wanted me to eat at his restaurant and take my money, but I don't get called beautiful that often. I want to feel like someone, I want to feel like a real person, so I soak in the rare compliment.

I leave the to-go box on an elevated top. I couldn't bring myself to throw it away, I wanted to leave it for someone or something. It's not my problem anymore.

...

I slept better. It was hard to fall asleep at first because of all the noises outside. Someone was screaming his head off maybe at midnight, I'm not sure. *Filho da puta!* He screamed. When I woke up, it was raining. The rain soothed me back to sleep. I curled into a ball under the covers and hugged myself for comfort. Staying on the fifth floor makes me feel disconnected from the world.

I finally decided to conquer the day and lifted the covers off. I don't have class today because of the carnival. In the communal bathroom, I bumped into someone. Before this morning, I hadn't seen any signs of life, and suspicions of being the only one on this floor had risen. It was relieving to see another person, and I felt less uneasy.

I threw some clothes on before walking down the stairs and going outside. The air is moist, and the streets are still wet from the rain. I'm mostly walking uphill, my legs feel heavy, and my lungs are working overtime. My right ear starts to hurt. I get sweaty, I take my jacket off, I get cold, I put the jacket back on. It's cloudy and it looks like it'll start raining again. Finally, I made it to Jardim da Estrela. I sit on one of the benches under the trees. All this greenery makes me happy.

I walk out of the park; I didn't stay long. My throat tightens and I become nauseous again. I want my mother, I want to run into her arms, I want to feel safe. Because she's on the other side of Europe, I feel the urge to take refuge in a church. I'm originally Evangelical Lutheran. However, I left the church *the day* I turned eighteen. I did believe at one point, well, I desperately wanted to believe. I couldn't fathom my existence, the universe, and the doom everything including me would experience. I wanted to have some faith that would help me deal with all my feelings that were too big for a child to have.

When I got older, I realized that I just needed to accept my existence and its temporariness. I never really believed. Thinking about my history with Christianity, it took me by surprise that I have the urge to seek shelter in a Catholic church. I see a church, and almost go inside, but it doesn't feel proper to do so. It doesn't feel correct to go to a Catholic church after being Evangelical Lutheran for eighteen years, or twenty years. I don't know if I stopped being a Christian after leaving the church, I don't think it works like that since I was baptized and did my confirmation.

The walk exhausted me. I lie on my bed staring at the ceiling. I'm tired, I should go to sleep since I have classes tomorrow. Well, fuck that, I'm not going to sleep because the fire alarm went off. I start throwing things into my bag: passport, wallet, charger, phone. I run to the door and just as I open it, the alarm stops. Two other people on my floor are standing with me in the hallway. We are confused. We look at each other without exchanging words. A security guard yells from the stairwell, *it's a false alarm*. Finally, we exchanged words each in our own native language, yet understanding what was needed; *everything was fine*. I return to my room shaking, I lie on the bed shaking so much that the bed starts to do the same.

…

After the alarm went off last night, it took me a while until I managed to fall asleep. When I finally dozed off, I slept well and woke up a few minutes before my alarm went off.

I'm walking to school, and I stop in front of a building. The outer walls are decorated with blue azulejos. I have that same patterned azulejo tattooed on my left arm. I take a photo of the azulejos, just like I did two years ago.

Our teacher is an older woman. She's a very good teacher. I feel like I'll start missing her. I get attached to strangers, and to people I've only known for short periods of my life. I know they don't remember me like I carry them in my memories.

After class, I head back to my room. My hips ache from yesterday's walking. I feel like my hips will disconnect from the rest of my skeleton, making me fall to the ground, and break my face. I lie on my bed after walking up the stairs. The bed is hard, and I can feel the bed springs dig into my bones. Every time I move, I feel like my bones will chip pieces off. I fell asleep and slept for almost an hour. I wake up with my legs still aching.

I ended up outside after dragging my ass up from the bed. I'm walking towards Miradouro de Santa Luzia. I don't have anything in my mind, I just feel like walking there. I see a church and know it feels *incorrect* to go inside one, but something in my gut screams at me to go in. As soon as I step inside the church, the smell becomes overwhelming. I'm scared to go further in. Slowly and carefully, I walk to sit on a bench. My heart is beating wildly, and my chest might become bruised on the inside. I look around, feeling small and insignificant. I feel like I'm being watched, so quickly and quietly I make my way out of the church. Someone catches me on the street and talks me into eating at their restaurant. I'm anxious, but a drink might help. I order a strawberry cheesecake and a caipirinha. I call my father; I want to hear his voice. I order another caipirinha. I call my younger brother; I want to know how he's doing. I get drunk fast; I feel more confident, and I leave a big tip. I'm happy, I feel like I'm home.

I'm quite drunk when I get back. I hurt my leg while opening the door to my room after trying to wave at the security camera which made me lose my balance, and I had to catch myself before hitting the floor.

People who work in this place I'm staying at, are the same ones who were here two years ago. I wasn't expecting to see them. They see hundreds of faces come and go, they won't remember me, but I'll remember them. I feel like a face belonging to them will pop up in my head instead of a loved one when I'm on my deathbed.

…

The alcohol made me sleepy, so I went to bed early. I keep my window open to have fresh air in my room, but all the noises are louder. This city doesn't sleep, and a loud noise woke me up. It was hard to fall back asleep because I had a hangover forming. The wind made its way to my room and caused my door to move. The noise from the door added to my difficulty in falling asleep. I pushed my suitcase against the door to keep it in place, but that proved useless.

I managed to fall asleep at some point and I woke up to rain violently hitting my window. During my ten-minute walk to school, I got soaked from head to toe. My shoes are so wet, and I can feel my toes turn ice cold to touch. It burns my toes, I don't feel anything, it burns again. My clothes feel like they've been glued onto my skin. I can't stand this feeling, it's making me insane, I want to pull my own skin off.

I couldn't concentrate well because of my hangover, but it's my fault for drinking. My wet clothes also made it more difficult; I could only think about the feeling of wet fabric on my skin. I make it back to my room and peel off my clothes. I throw my shoes off not caring where they land. I hang some of my clothes to dry before unpacking my bag and putting my grammar book on the bed. I have a test tomorrow and want to do well on it. I don't like studying grammar, however, when it's the grammar of a language you're interested in, it makes the experience more tolerable. Two years ago, I studied the same topic in grammar, so it's slowly coming back to me as I revise and study.

I don't know for how long I've studied, but sunlight sneaks into my room. It feels like a warm blanket around me. I throw my book back on the table and put on my shoes which are still a little bit wet.

Miradouro de São Pedro de Alcântara, that's where I ended up. This is my favorite viewpoint in Lisbon, and I always come here whenever I'm in the city. The view takes my breath away. The castle, Castelo de São Jorge, always captivates my gaze. The castle sits on a hill looking down at the city like a guardian. I order a caipirinha and sit down on the benches, staring at the castle. I don't know for how long I sat there before noticing dark clouds coming closer. I don't want to get soaked again.

There are vendors selling all kinds of things: food, jewelry, drinks. I can't help but look at the jewelry. I don't wear any, yet somehow, I had been thinking about buying myself a bracelet. One bracelet caught my eye. I remember one of my old classmates at the language school years ago had a similar one. I have been thinking about that bracelet for almost two years. I buy the bracelet and ask the vendor to help me put it on my wrist, and he does just that. *Muito obrigada*, I told him before running off never to be seen again by him.

I was walking towards my accommodation, but I ended up in a restaurant somewhere near Largo do Carmo. Between the buildings, the castle peeks through. I stare at the castle and feel like the castle stares back at me.

…

I had a strange dream full of familiar faces. I don't remember much, but I saw an old colleague of mine, and when she called me in the dream my alarm went off, and I woke up. This was the first time that my alarm managed to take me by surprise. I did an early check-in for my flight tomorrow, and I feel blue. I don't want to leave, but at the same time, I miss my dog. I hope she isn't mad at me that I've been gone for a week.

I walk into the classroom and the teacher announces that we'll have the test right now. While doing the test, I feel extremely anxious. I want to do well; I want the teacher to know that I'm good. After the test, I needed to catch my breath, so I sat outside the classroom for ten minutes while the teacher was looking through our tests. It humbled me, but I got a B- and I think that grade is acceptable for someone who was mostly hungover some days, and last studied grammar properly two years ago. The class ended as soon as it started, and a C1 certificate landed in my hands. *A fourth one to add to my collection.*

Holy hell, the walk up to the castle always kills me, but I had to do it. It's my third time inside these castle walls. I touch the wall with my index finger, and it feels cold. A piece of history that has existed long before me and will continue to exist after I cease to be. I climb up the walls and my legs feel weak because I'm slightly scared of heights. I stumble and almost fall down, however, I wouldn't be mad if I cracked my head open in a place like this. Carefully, I come down the uneven stairs and continue walking around. A sign catches my attention: *archeological site.* My head fills with joy as I gallop like an excited child, only slowing my pace to not scare the peacocks. Ruins, I see ruins. I wish I could get closer to them and touch them. The other visitors look at me funny, and I think I'm smiling like an idiot. Finally, I return to the entrance and sit down in the same exact spot where I sat at fifteen years old. A pigeon comes to sit near me, and I wave at the bird.

I'm stuffing my face with pasta. The pasta has bacon, tomato sauce, cheese, and pepper. I haven't eaten anything properly during my time here, so this pasta feels heavenly in my mouth and stomach. I wash it all down with a caipirinha. I think all these caipirinhas will catch up to me when I get older. Probably by the time I'm thirty.

I drag myself up the stairs to my room for the last time. I'm already feeling homesick, and I haven't left Lisbon yet. I start sobbing on the bed. This is not an unusual reaction.

After a few minutes of sobbing and thrashing on the bed like a lunatic, I calm myself down.

…

During the night there was an extremely loud sound. The sound started quietly in the distance, but I knew as it came closer that the sound would be *loud*. As the sound hit, I had to muffle my ears with a pillow. I curled into myself under the blanket. I thought the sky was falling on me. The sound came and went, yet my fast heartbeat continued. From the street, I heard a man yell while laughing: *what the fuck was that?* I fell asleep soon after and had strange dreams that I no longer remember.

After I woke up, I took one last shower in the communal bathrooms, and I noticed the black dots on the ceiling of the shower. *Mold.* Well, that explains my scratchy throat now and then.

The airport feels suffocating. I still have three hours before boarding starts, so I should try to find something to eat. I made it through security without getting into an additional search which was surprising. Finally, inside the plane, I get a whole row to myself. 19A lucky once again. We rise in the air and head towards Northern Europe. I order a non-alcoholic drink, and I use hand sanitizer before opening my bag of chips. Due to the pressure in the plane, the hand sanitizer pops open and some of it flies in my eye. I curse and curse, I might go blind.

CONSEQUENCES

Running from fate is useless, and I know the barricaded door of this weak shed won't hold. A priest, bless his soul, tried to bargain with her to spare me. Religion has blinded him; he believed everyone deserves forgiveness yet his God would strike me down. A rational individual knows that a violent end is justified for people like *me*. An eerie howl shakes the rotting shed I'm hiding in, and my gut knows she's close. It won't be long until she forces her way through the barricade and takes what I no longer deserve.

She slams against the barricaded door, tearing it open in one swift motion. The moonlight illuminates the dark shed, giving me a clear view of her in front of me. A tall, looming beast with fur as black as midnight, and glowing red eyes. The gigantic dog opens her mouth, revealing sharp canines. Pleading and begging won't work, but I still try. She wastes no time and lunges at my neck.

PANTS...?

The 'castle' overlooks the town full of farmers, trying to make it through a rough life. Locals have gone missing under suspicious circumstances over the last centuries. Children speak of a tall figure crawling up walls into houses and taking victims away, never to be seen again. Parents tell their children not to speak of the malevolent forces. God is watching over them, according to the locals, at least.

...

"Ah, yes, I've heard about this *tale*." Mr. Kalis says, holding the teacup close to his face. The table has been set with decorated dishes full of varying delicacies, and silverware. His guests, Mr. Greene and Henderson, are sitting across the table, enjoying a warm cup of tea.

"Is this tale, *made up* by children, the reason you've come all the way from Ireland?" Mr. Kalis asks, putting his cup down. His eyes are the lightest green the two investigators have seen in their lives, and Mr. Kalis' intense gaze catches them off guard. "Gentlemen, is everything alright?"

"Yes, my apologies," Mr. Henderson manages. "Well, the children are quite adamant about this story. Children rarely lie."

"We spoke with various children and your home came up every time, Mr. Kalis." The other investigator continues.

"Please, you can call me Marlow," Mr. Kalis, Marlow, laughs. "I can understand why. My home is an old manor, and children are known to have wild imaginations, I'm sure you are aware of that."

"Of course," Mr. Greene chuckles. "But as investigators, we have to look into every lead."

"Oh, yes, I do understand that. Whatever you need, I'm here to help. I want the townsfolk to be safe." Marlow replies, smiling.

…

After Mr. Greene and Henderson were shown to their bed chambers, Marlow made his way toward the lowest floor of the manor. A flame is never needed to guide him, Mr. Kalis knows the building like the back of his hand. The walls of his home are cold to touch, the same temperature as his body. Marlow opens the heavy door without difficulty and finally lights a candle, not for visibility but for ambience. He ignores the crying and thrashing man in the corner and lets his hair free. Marlow's hair is wavy, raven-colored, and shoulder-length. He opens his tight suit jacket, revealing a feminine figure.

"These *men* are a little too close to my liking," Marlow says to the captive man. "They want me to help find the crawling individual. It's funny, right?"

The man begins to trash violently. Thankfully, his sobbing is muffled by the gag she put on him. The man's panic makes her hungry, and swiftly Marlow appears behind him. Her fangs sink into his neck. She sucks his blood, feeding her craving, until the captive stops moving. *It wasn't as good as the last one*, Marlow thinks to herself, wiping her jaw of his vital fluid. She inspects the corpse, thinking of a way to dispose of it.

…

"Morning, gentlemen!" Marlow says as the investigators appear at the prepared table. "My husband had to attend to some business, so I'll be taking care of you today."

"Mr. Kalis never mentioned he was married." Mr. Greene says, surprised.

"Oh, how silly of him. He can be a bit forgetful at times," she laughs. "Please, sit down and enjoy."

"Does your husband approve of... This?" Mr. Henderson asks when she walks by toward the kitchen.

"What do you mean, Mr. Henderson?"

"His wife wearing... Pants." Mr. Greene replies.

"I assure you he's fine with it," she smiles. "In fact, he insists."

Silence follows her statement. The men look at her suspiciously. She doesn't know the extent of their investigations or skills, yet she's anxious to find out, and have some fun with them.

"Sausage made by my husband," she points at their plates. "And bread baked by me." Mr. Henderson wastes no time, stuffing his face full of food. The man eats like he hasn't for years. On the other hand, Mr. Greene is more hesitant to try the food. She notices his hand slowly reaching toward his pocket.

"*Stop it*," she commands. The men freeze in place, unable to move their bodies according to their will. She's their master now. "I was going to drag this out for longer, but I don't like not knowing what you're reaching for." She gets up from her chair, walks over to Mr. Greene, and searches his pockets to find a tiny bottle of holy water. "You're good, I'll give you that, Mr. Greene."

"*Speak*," she commands. The men are still glued to their seats, but now able to use their mouths.

"Did you kill Mr. Kalis?" Mr. Henderson asks.

"No?" She says, confused. "I'm Mr. Kalis."

"That's impossible." He replies.

"It's really not, I can be both. You could see that if you two weren't so... What's the word? Ah! *Old-fashioned*."

"You're tricking us!" Mr. Greene growls.

"How am I doing that?" She inquires. "*Oh*, well, in a way I am, but it's not the biggest problem for you right now."

"You've killed Mr. Kalis to take his place," Mr. Greene tries to move, but can't. "You're the reason for every disappearance."

"You're correct, I'm behind the missing townsfolk, but Mr. Kalis is alive because I'm him. He's me and I'm him, it's really not that complicated."

"I don't believe your devilish words!" He spews.

"Can a man not be evil? Does a woman have to be the only evil, is that what you're saying?" Marlow appears right beside Mr. Greene, her face is centimeters apart from his. "You looked me in the eyes yesterday, they're the same ones you're looking into now. *Good morning, Thomas Greene.*" She lowers her voice to match Mr. Kalis'. The investigator's eyes widened in shock.

"Your latest victim," Mr. Henderson whispers. "Is he alive? The preacher?"

"You ate him," Marlow responds. "So, no, he's not alive."

"*Devil!*" One of them screams.

"That's not very nice, fellas." Marlow sighs. She appears behind Mr. Henderson and bites his neck. He shrieks and starts reciting prayers. The words burn her ears, so she resorts to snapping his neck, killing him instantly.

"*Quiet,*" she commands when Mr. Greene begins to yell his prayers. "Your friend did not taste good. Maybe because he stuffed his fat throat full of that preacher." Marlow pushes the corpse out of the chair, making it hit the cold ground of her manor. The fall created an eerie sound that echoed inside the old building. She wonders what to do with the remaining investigator.

"Do you have a family, Thomas?" Marlow inquires. "Just move your eyes from side to side if you don't."

"I don't think you do. I doubt he had one either." She answers her own question. She appears behind him, placing her hands on his shoulders. Marlow wraps her cold hands around his warm throat, feeling his erratic heartbeat. "I won't eat you, don't worry. *I'll send your corpse back to Dublin.*" She squeezes with all her strength, breaking his neck in the process.

FOREST FAIRIES

She didn't notice the sun setting; the photographer had gotten lost in her little world. Now, she's cursing to herself leaning against a tree in the dark. She's somewhere she shouldn't be, she had walked off trail in the natural park. The photographer isn't good with orientation, she doesn't know which way south or which way is north, also she's missing a physical map, making her predicament more irritating. She won't be lost forever; someone will find her eventually or she'll find someone. The volcanic island isn't big, if she goes south, she might end up in Furnas or Povoação. She sighs, annoyed and tired, but tries to work out her whereabouts on her phone, yet her electronic device is unable to locate her. "Fuck," she mumbles. "Piece of shit never works." The photographer decides to head north, at least she thinks she's heading north. She's going uphill, downhill, uphill, sideways on a steep slope, uphill, sideways on a steep slope again, uphill, downhill. Confused, she sits down on a rock, still within the trees. The silent trees stare at her, she knows if they'd possess mouths, laughter will erupt and break the quiet night.

She had closed her eyes, half-asleep, until the sound of distant humming made her alert. The sound captivates every living thing on the island. Eyes wide and heart beating wildly, she gets up from the rock. The photographer grips the small flashlight in her hands as she follows the ancient-sounding song. The humming gets stronger, she realizes that many voices are mixing. In the distance, she sees a small white dot illuminating trees. Three people are circling the dot, it's a strange, they move as if gravity doesn't exist. Slowly, she takes her camera out and takes a photo, then another photo, a third one, a fourth, and a fifth one—

"Blasphemous!" A hand pulls the photographer's arm down; she almost drops the expensive camera. Her heart stops beating for a second, and dread takes over her whole being, wondering who she's up against in the dark forest. The photographer doesn't feel like becoming the next headline in newspapers. She glares at the person covered by darkness and steps away from the unknown assailant.

"Why are you intruding on our practices?" The voice asked. The photographer shines her flashlight toward the high-pitched voice revealing a short naked woman. Fear and anticipation are replaced with confusion and amusement.

"Why are you naked?" The photographer asks dumbfounded. "I think that's a better question."

"You didn't answer *my* question, heathen." The naked woman has an accent. She steps closer to the photographer; she backs away from the woman just to get stopped by a pair of arms encircling her from behind.

"Hey, what the fuck? Get off me!" She starts struggling against the arms around her but she's fighting against iron. The naked woman standing before her grabs the camera. The arms around her belong to a woman, she can feel the other assailants' breasts press into her back. It makes the photographer unsettled.

"Answer to Sister Ceres," the woman behind her demands.

"Fuck! I got lost, okay?" The photographer spits.

"Don't use such language around divine beings," Ceres, the short naked woman says. "Can't you show basic respect?"

"Get off me and I might be nicer," the trapped woman snarls. "Seriously, what the hell is this?"

"What is your name?" Ceres interrogates.

"Mariana," the photographer replies. "Do you fucking mind letting me go?"

"Mariana, do you understand that you've angered the deities?" The woman holding her hostage asks.

"Hush, Diana, she doesn't need to know." Ceres sternly replies.

"What are you talking about?" Mariana turns her head to stare at Diana, the woman whose arms are wrapped around her tightly.

"Augusta! Elysia!" Ceres yells. It doesn't take long for two pairs of running footsteps to reach the three women. With the small amount of light coming from the photographer's flashlight, she can make out two tall naked women standing behind Ceres. "At least you guys aren't naked men." Mariana mutters, trying her luck once more with Diana.

"I'm guessing these two are Augusta and Elysia?" Mariana inquires. The two women standing behind Ceres stay silent and still like statues.

"You're coming with us," Diana says to the captive woman.

"To fucking civilization, I hope." She begins her struggle again but stops when she notices Ceres giving one of the taller women in front of her a wooden stick.

"Do it, Augusta," Ceres commands. Diana lets go of Mariana just in time for Augusta to hit her head with the wooden stick. The stick might as well be a rock; it knocks the photographer out cold and she falls to the side, hitting her head again. She's dragged by her ankles toward the white light, but the dancers around it have stopped long ago.

A splash of water wakes Mariana up; she's tied to a tree. The rough rope digs into her skin. Her head hurts, and the flashlight shoved into her face makes the pain worse. Water managed to slip into her lungs, causing her to start coughing violently.

"She interrupted the ritual," *Diana*. "We need to start preparations all over again!"

"Do not let a lower being anger you like this." An unknown woman says. Her accent sounds Northern American.

"Of course, lady Venus," Diana replies with an embarrassed tone. The flashlight is finally removed from her face, and Mariana blinks, trying to get used to the sudden change. She looks around, and there are more than the four women who knocked her out. She counts *nine* women in total.

"You, heathen, what is your purpose here?" Augusta, the woman who knocked her out, asks.

"I already told you jackasses: I got lost." Mariana mumbles. The piercing pain in her head causes dizziness and the women in front of her to double in amount.

"See? She cannot speak with respect." Ceres says.

"I see what you mean," the woman with the American accent responds. Mariana thinks she's *Lady Venus*.

"What will we do with her?" Diana raises her voice, clearly irritated.

"Why are you all naked?" Mariana looks around. She should find out why she had been tied to a tree, but no, finding out why her captors are naked is more important.

"You cannot comprehend the reason, so there's no use in telling you." A short haired, plump woman responds.

"Pax, quiet." A bald woman with a British accent, commands. The short haired woman, Pax, immediately bows her head down in submission.

"We'll handle this, all I ask is that you stand guard and do not let more heathens step onto our holy ground," Venus says and places a hand on the bald woman's shoulder. "Mars, my love, please speak with Jupiter and Terra for me. I'll interrogate this outsider." The bald one, Mars, nods and places a gentle kiss on Venus' cheek. Mariana is disturbed by the nine naked women with strange names.

"I just got lost, Venus—" a hand swiftly meets her cheek. It makes her vision go white for a second.

"It is *Lady Venus* to you," Venus herself hisses at Mariana.

"Okay, I apologize, my mistake," she mutters after gaining her composure back. "*Lady* Venus, I just got lost. I don't want anything to do with your practices, I can promise you that."

"I don't believe you." Pax growls.

"Well, I don't think *you* get to decide that fatass. I noticed your strange little hierarchy." Mariana can't stop herself from hurling insults. Another slap lands on her cheek. This time it came from Mars.

"Such foul language," the bald woman sighs. "Our deities aren't happy with it."

"Can you stop hitting me, please?" The photographer pleads.

"Be more respectful if you wish not to get hurt," Venus replies.

"Fine, I'm sorry. Is that better?" The bound woman sighs. The weak light illuminates Mars' smirk, and it makes Mariana furious. She wants to wipe the ground with her smirk.

"How did you find us, Mariana?" Venus' face comes closer to hers.

"I got lost, I didn't exactly find your, uh, holy ground." She says.

"Uh-huh, why did you take photos of our deities?" An unknown woman asks who also has an American accent.

"I'm a photographer and I'm working on my portfolio—"

"I don't need your whole life story," the mystery woman cuts her off. "Why our deities?"

"It looked beautiful, I take photos of beautiful things. Does this answer please you ladies?"

"It's not meant for your camera lens or your eyes." Mars growls.

"I'm sorry, I can delete the photos," Mariana suggests. "Can you untie me? I just need to get to Achada."

"No," the mystery woman says. "You cannot leave."

...

Gentle morning light wakes her up. *What a strange dream,* she thinks to herself, but the throbbing pain in her head makes her aware of reality. She looks around; the women are sleeping. Mariana notices that there are only five sleeping bags, the so-called 'ladies' aren't there. She sees Pax, the short-haired woman she insulted, lying on her back with her eyes closed. The sleeping bag isn't covering her fully and she sees that they've finally decided to put some clothes on. Quietly, Mariana tries her luck with the rope tying her to the tree. It's not loose but it's not tight either. She squirms around until one of the sleeping women wakes up, Ceres.

"You're awake, heathen." She smiles at Mariana. The photographer doesn't respond and just glares at one of her captors. "Not in the mood to talk? You were spouting all kinds of obscenities only a few hours ago."

"I'm tired, my head hurts, and I'm tied to a damn tree. So, no I'm not in the mood to talk." Ceres stays silent. She gets up and wakes the other women up.

"Morning ritual and then breakfast, you know how it goes sisters," Ceres says when all of them have rolled their sleeping bags up. The five women gather in a circle and hold each other's hands, they start rambling in *very* bad Latin. Mariana can't help her curious nature; she observes their perplexing actions and takes mental notes. Once they stop speaking Latin—it can't be called Latin—Pax removes herself from the circle and goes to a picnic basket sitting near the tree where she's tied up. Pax takes a bag of white powder that she brings to her sisters. *I've been kidnapped by a violent gang of odd crackheads,* the photographer starts getting anxious and tugs on her bindings. One of the women, Augusta, notices her distress and signals her sisters to pay attention to their captive.

"Stop what you're doing, heathen," Ceres commands.

"Can you just let me go, please?" She pleads. Ceres shakes her head. "Oh, fuck you all!" Mariana shouts and starts thrashing around but stops when her headache gets worse. The women stare at her in amusement.

"What will we do with this one?" Diana asks.

"The ladies are discussing it," Ceres responds. "They're speaking with the deities tonight." Mariana decides to stay quiet; she can't deal with their craziness right now.

The women eat breakfast, dried fruits and peanuts. Mariana hates peanuts, but she would do anything for sustenance. If they'd tell her to do cartwheels to get food, she'd do it. Her stomach keeps growling, the women notice it, but they don't offer her anything. "Can I get water, please? Just a sip, I'm dying over here." She pleads. Diana rolls her eyes, but Ceres gives her a stern look which makes her rummage through the picnic basket. She holds Mariana's half-full water bottle that she had with her.

"Thank you," the photographer says. "I appreciate it." Diana opens the bottle, and brings it closer to the bound woman, but ultimately, she just swings the bottle making water splash on her face. The other women laugh, but Ceres gives Diana a death stare.

"That was uncalled for," she says to Diana. "Let her drink, we cannot let her die without the approval of our deities."

"What, are you going to sacrifice me to some fucking forest fairies?" Mariana continues her squirming.

"Do not speak ill of our deities!" Augusta roars.

"I already did, what are you going to do? Hit me with a fucking stick again?"

"You will regret your poorly chosen words," Augusta growls. "I will not stand for blasphemy."

"Kill yourselves, how about that?" The photographer's words make all the women angry; they step closer to her. Augusta looks like she'll strangle her to death. Diana is about to pounce on her when all of them start hearing the same humming that led to Mariana finding them, and the sisters back off. The ladies appear in the distance and behind them are three other women.

"Oh, great, there's twelve of you lunatics."

"Shut your mouth, this is your last warning," Ceres whispers harshly. The sisters get on their knees when the ladies step to the side revealing the three women, *naked women*. The humming continues until the blonde unknown naked woman raises her hand to signal them to stop. Mariana stares at them with wide eyes.

"I, Solstice, greet you on behalf of the stars," the blonde one says with a thick French accent. "What is your name?" She points at Mariana.

"Mariana but I think you weirdos already knew that." The ladies glare at her, but Solstice smiles ear to ear.

"No, I mean your true name."

"It's Mariana," she says unamused.

"It is not," Solstice argues.

"Okay, *Solstice*, what is my true name? Since you know everything."

"Altalune," she raises her hands toward the sky. "You will serve the moon greatly. We must keep her happy."

"Jesus Christ, what are you girls on?" Mariana almost yells.

"Now, now, Altalune. We, the stars, will guide you." Solstice tries to calm the captive down.

"Don't call me that," Mariana hisses. "It's not my name. I'm not a servant of the fucking moon, and you're not stars. What kind of drugs do you do? Can I get some so we're on the same page."

"It's the greatest honor to serve the moon."

"No, no, no, stop." Mariana starts thrashing around violently.

"Venus, my daughter, prepare Altalune for tonight's full moon. We'll take care of the rest." Solstice commands.

It's nighttime again; Mariana had been left alone by the women. She's shivering. Venus drenched her in water, and she said that it was a part of the ritual. She didn't want any details from her captor. She only cursed and yelled insults. The photographer squirms around; she can feel the rope getting looser and looser. She continues until her left wrist slips free. The stiffness of her arm is uncomfortable, but getting feeling back to one's limbs is wonderful. It takes a few minutes for her to be able to free the remaining wrist. She gets up from the ground on shaky legs. Mariana goes through the picnic basket; she finds her camera, wallet, phone, and flashlight, and some white powder she decides to not take. She stills her movements to listen to the forest around her, it would tell where the women were. Mariana decides to run off to the direction her heart tells her to. Each running step makes her head throb worse, but it's the least of her worries. Her flashlight and the moon she's supposed to serve give her enough light not to run into anything. She slows her pace to catch her breath and leans against a tree to stabilize her shaking body.

When she's regained some strength back, she gets back to running. In the distance behind her, she hears a shriek. It belongs to one of the women. The naked women must have parted ways to investigate the whole small forest to find her. She picks up speed, but her feet trip on something. Mariana falls face first on the ground, and the force of her fall makes her headache spread all over her body. Her vision spins like she's drunk. The photographer lies on the ground for a moment before forcing herself up, she looks behind her to make sure that Ceres or fatass Pax isn't standing there. They aren't, but she feels something with her foot. It must be the thing that tripped her. She touches it, it's another picnic basket. Mariana puts her flashlight in between her teeth and opens the basket. She finds clothes and a wallet. She opens the wallet and finds an ID inside. She takes the card and puts it in her pocket before kicking the basket over. The shrieks in the distance get louder, and she takes off running again.

Mariana sees the edge of the forest. She's never been a runner, but she keeps going even if her feet are begging for mercy. The sun is starting to rise. She gets out of the tiny, beautiful hellhole and continues to run. The body collapses in exhaustion when she's able to see the ocean in the distance. The lovely moist breeze on her face makes her body relax, but she still hears the shrieks. Mariana weakly gets on her hands and knees and starts moving forward. She looks up and sees a lone house further away, and it makes her motivation rise to the clouds.

"Altalune, why are you running?" *Solstice.* Her head drops down and she can see a pair of bare feet walking behind her.

"Fuck off," Mariana mumbles. "Stop this divine religious spiritual bullshit or whatever it is."

"I can forgive your shortcomings, but only if you speak more respectfully about the stars. I'm the brightest being in this universe."

"Your real name is Emma, behave yourself." Mariana says. Solstice stops dead in her tracks, but Mariana continues her journey toward the house.

"What–"

"You heard me, Emma."

"How did you find out my earthly name?" Emma is frantic.

"I tripped over a fucking basket; I found your stupid wallet. It's ugly as shit, get a better one. I'm begging you. Solstice what an idiotic name." Mariana hurls insult after insult, it's the only thing making her feel like she's the one winning when she's crawling on the muddy ground.

"Isn't this forest protected by the government or something? You call it your holy land, but in reality, you're just being an asshole, and littering." Emma stays silent and lets Mariana crawl further away.

"You aren't special, and you don't get to hold people hostage in a forest, a really fucking beautiful forest, which is a damn shame. Get out of there, it doesn't belong to you idiots." Mariana doesn't know what she's saying anymore, she only wants to hurt Emma's feelings. It's all she's able to do.

"I think it's time to get a job, put on some clothes, and stop doing drugs in the forest." The photographer reaches the backyard of the house; she turns around to see if Emma is following her. She only sees her walking uphill back into the forest naked as the day she was born.

...

Mariana sits by the boarding gate with her head bandaged up. Her sunglasses cover dark eyebags. She looks through her camera. Photos of cows, Ponta Delgada, Mosteiros, the natural park where she got lost, and the dark photo of the 'deities' dancing around the flashlight. She turns the camera off and places it into her bag. She lies back on the airport seats, they're uncomfortable and remind her of the cold ground she sat on for a few days.

When boarding starts, Mariana rushes to get inside the plane among the first passengers. She walks to the back of the plane and takes her window seat, she puts her belongings in the overhead compartment, and under the seat in front of her. An older man sits on the aisle seat and acknowledges his seatmate with a small smile. Mariana closes her eyes and hopes that the next time she opens them she's back home.

"Excuse me, I'm sitting in the middle." The familiar voice makes the photographer's heart drop. She removes her sunglasses and stares at the woman who's talking with the man in the aisle seat. "Emma?"

COVEN

In the darkness, I tried to force my paralyzed body to move, even a twitch of my finger could've kept my hopes up. Thoughts of despair raced through my mind, so strong they were. Bodies stuck to my naked flesh, bodily fluids acting as glue. The smell is nauseating; however, I'd become used to it.

I was the only one still possessing a heartbeat, the rest had lost theirs long ago. My organ became violent in its fight to survive, during moments when it slowed down, I feared my time was up.

My hair stuck to my face. Sticky, sweaty, and wet, foreign locks on my bare skin drove me to the edge of insanity. Dead and cold limbs once so full of life pressed deep into my muscles, a ghastly remainder of my similar fate.

From darkness I came, to darkness I left, yet the last thing I wished to see was something delicate, beautiful, and bright. I fear the dead laugh at my childish hopes, mocking me while taking hold of my spirit to pull me out of this world.

ELEVATOR INCIDENT OF 2016

Before stepping into that elevator my mind was sharp. I felt like I could see everything: my boss' new hair, my coworker's hidden sour mood, the food stains on our janitor's dark uniform, or the dirt on our office windows. I was a different person. I was kind, thoughtful, and hardworking Joana. The elevator was empty, and it wasn't as bright as the office. The small box was like another dimension. Suddenly, there was a transparent wall between my eyes and brain. It appeared out of thin air and I couldn't get rid of it. My hands were no longer my own; they seemed alien. It was someone else who stepped inside the elevator; that was Joana. At this moment, I'm another Joana. Seconds into the future, once again, I'm another Joana.

The elevator walls were mirrors. I could see myself and another person inside the box whom I hadn't noticed before. She must've been another coworker of mine. We stood in silence as the elevator descended down the skyscraper. I felt myself being anxious, yet the feeling wasn't inside me. A transparent shield around me kept it away from penetrating my body, but it still surrounded me. It felt suffocating. I wanted the transparent walls gone.

Maybe I needed to cause a collision between force fields. My coworker with her pale, almost white skin stood in place as I eyed her, desperate. Like a child biting into fresh snow, my teeth sunk into her flesh. Warm liquid dripping down my mouth, I took another bite of her. She didn't scream, beg, or fight. She let me collide our shields. Perhaps, she knew what I was feeling and was also troubled. We just wanted to help each other.

Hands grabbing my arms, stopped me from biting into her. My boss held my left arm, and a security guard held my right arm tightly. I saw my boss' mouth moving, she looked frantic as she pressed something on my wrist. I noticed the blood pooling by our feet. The blood around my mouth was already drying, and it started to itch. My boss yelled something along the lines of *what the fuck Joana* and *why the hell did you bite your wrist open*. She's mistaken; I bit my coworker. Maybe the transparent shield is confusing her reality. I opened my mouth to advise her of my remedy for freedom, but a piece of flesh dropped from my mouth. It landed in the puddle. My boss and the security guard let my arms free and backed away with horror. I bring my wrist back to my mouth and bite down.

GOD HAS BEAUTIFUL EYES

She imagined twirling around her fingers the curly chestnut hair of the woman she loved. She remembered the softness of *her* hair against bare skin. The nights they shared under the stars were the happiest of her life. Only the moon and stars knew of what they had. She formed a deep hatred for the sun, when it rose, and people awoke, the women had to hide what they had. She wanted to spend the rest of her life, staring into the endless space that was her eyes. The sleepless nights were worth it. For some time, she was the luckiest woman alive.

She imagined the ropes, digging into her skin were the soft hands of her lover. They pulled, dislocating her joints. She pretended the pulsating warmth around her wrists was the heartbeat of her dearest, yet deep down she knew it was her torn skin, wetting the ropes red. She could stop this, confess her sins, and her accomplice. The woman could repent and try to save herself, that was what the men said. God for men was a beast, it only served them.

She had met God; kissed her lips, stared into her eyes, held her hands, and towered over her. She lived and breathed for her God. Gladly and with love, she would keep these animals away from her savior.

I WISH I WOULD

The young woman thought she could handle it for four months, and the money would be worth it. A *little* above minimum-wage, that was all she got for freezing in the horrid winter of Northern Finland, but it was enough to change her direction in life. The darkness was overwhelming, and she cherished the short hours of sunlight that kept her sane. It was a struggle getting out of bed every morning, and this day was no different. The thick blanket and pajamas weren't enough to shield from the cold. She shivered as she hugged the stuffed pig closer, fighting back the urge to quit her job, and curl deeper under covers never to be seen again.

She regretted leaving her home even if it was temporary; she missed the place she was born and raised in. It was a depressing place with its grey apartment buildings, rusting train stations, and unapproachable population. She wasn't welcome here; the people were *too* trusting and kind. She couldn't change the doubt that was drilled into her back home, and she didn't want to get rid of it. *Doubt* was something that kept a woman alive.

She cleaned the dirty hotel room, erasing every trace of the previous guests. A group of young men, maybe older than her, had stayed there for a week. She tried avoiding them, yet it was an impossible task in the small hotel. She thought about their lives: what did they do for a living, how did they treat others, and if they had any ambitions. As a cleaner, she had learned to figure out guests' personalities based on how they left their room. If a guest left the room tidy, the guest was compassionate. If a guest left it trashed, she knew the guest was an asshole. Life was never black and white, but this situation had to be an exception.

She moved on to the next room, noticed the *do not disturb* sign and left it alone. Another dirty room, she sighed and entered it. She played the music louder in her headphones, shutting the world out. It helped her to ignore the overwhelming empty feeling in her chest and aching back that interfered with her job. She vacuumed, changed sheets, wiped mirrors, and took the trash out.

It was snowing again. She cursed under her breath and wrapped the thin hoodie around herself tighter. A part of her wanted to lie down outside and let snow cover her, returning her to nature. The other part of her wanted to leave this godforsaken place and travel for warmer days. She missed the sun. The burning orb in the sky was the only thing that made sense to her. She felt they were similar; alone yet comfortable with it.

The next room was still occupied by someone. She gave the guest new towels, more toilet paper, and took the trash out. She began changing the sheets, and the blanket revealed the hiding spot of a familiar stuffed *pig*. It looked older and more worn than her own. She made the bed and gently placed the pig between the pillows, making it the king of its castle. She tapped the stuffed toy's head like she did to hers before leaving for her shift every day.

The guest came back to the room as she was leaving. She was an older woman, maybe in her late forties with some grey hairs matching her eyes. She wore glasses with silvery rims.

"Oh! Morning, I was just leaving." She said to the guest.

"Morning, thank you so much." The woman smiled and stepped out of the way for her to leave the room. She noticed the two beauty marks under her left eye, she had the same ones. On her break, she ate at the hotel's almost empty restaurant. The sun was setting and soon, her shift would end. Only two more months of this and she'd be on the train, going back home.

The day had exhausted her. She returned to the restaurant and sat down at the bar, ordering a vodka soda. She no longer needed to show her ID to the bartenders since she was basically a regular. One or two drinks after her shift was an unhealthy reward, yet she needed it to keep going. Giving up was always an option, yet the idea of returning home early bothered her even if she hated her temporary life.

"Mind if I sit here?" A familiar voice pulled her out of her head. The older woman whose room she had cleaned earlier stood there, waiting for a response.

"Sure, I don't mind." She said, confused why the other chose to sit right beside her in the empty bar. The woman ordered a non-alcoholic apple cider.

"I like how you positioned the pig on my bed," the woman started. "It was cute."

"I have the same pig, so I felt it was my duty." She replied.

"What a coincidence. Where'd you get yours?"

"Honestly, I don't know. My father got it for me when I was a baby." She tried remembering but to no avail. "I have this memory of him telling me, and it bothers me that I can't remember."

"You'll remember someday." The woman said.

"What about yours?"

"A similar story, but I finally remembered." The guest smiled. The older woman had her sleeves rolled up, revealing tattoos the younger also had on her covered arms.

"Why won't you leave this shithole?" The woman asked. "I still hate this place years later. I see it in my dreams."

"I'm not sure." She said, terrified and intrigued. They were alone, the bartender had disappeared, and the lights were flickering. "It's– it's just four months."

"This is the worst place you'll ever experience," the older one confessed. "It sucks your soul out. It's not for you."

"I need the money." The younger one argued.

"You can get money anywhere."

"It's just four months, I can handle it." The younger woman muttered.

"You're choosing to rot here just for money that will be gone the moment it hits your bank account?" The older woman leaned in closer. "Remember university?"

"I fucking hated that city." The younger one admitted.

"Yeah, and *we left*. Why won't you leave now?"

"I don't get it," she sighed. "It's just four months."

"Every time you feel overwhelmed, you'll remember this: drinking yourself soft after a shift in the middle of nowhere. Every negative feeling you'll experience in your life will be associated with this place. *Cold and isolated*, that's how you'll always feel."

She stared at herself; an older and experienced woman with some light left in her eyes. A part of her had already made its home here, and when she leaves, it'll stay. The part held her happiness before coming here, and it'll be here until the day of reckoning if she doesn't take the opportunity by the throat when it's handed to her.

Unmake me.

She was dropped on a beach she had visited years ago. She sat made herself comfortable on the warm sand, feeling the gentle breeze caress her cheeks. The sun was shining down relentlessly. Her body was on fire, her skin was turning bright red, and peeling. Surprisingly, it wasn't agonizing, slowly being burned to death by sunlight. Her skin fell off, muscles shrunk, and bones started poking through. It didn't take long until only a skeleton was left. The structured bones crumbled, landing and rolling into a puddle. She'd already left as her skin started melting.

She woke up on a moving train, confused and slightly hungover. Her bag was by her feet, and she was dressed in thick winter clothes. The wagon was otherwise empty aside from a few lonely passengers. As the train came to a stop, she looked out the window to see a familiar face walk by. The older woman smiled and waved at her before disappearing into the parking lot by the small town's station.

EVELYN

"He disobeyed orders," the voice on the phone paused. "You two know what happens to those who don't do as they're told, right?" The pair tasked with the job of taking out their senior, *Four*, exchanged looks before One hummed in agreement. "Do we already know his whereabouts?" Seven, the younger of the two, asked. Their senior was the organisation's most skilled operative with over twenty successful jobs under his belt.

"Our latest information confirmed that he's staying at his ex-wife's house." The voice responded. Before One could open her mouth, the call ended.

"Do we need to kill him inside his ex-wife's house?" Seven looked at his partner, dismayed. "That's really fucked up."

"The boss is—"

"A huge fucking cunt?"

"Exactly," One sighed. "Is there a worse word to describe our employer?"

"We'd be here all night, listing every possible offensive name." Seven slumped into the passenger seat.

"The dude just wants to retire," Seven rubbed his face with his hands. "This is so unfair."

"We're going to get killed by our so-called colleagues, too." One said.

"Oh, God, I hope they don't send Three or Zero after us," Seven laughed. "I hate those two. I wish they'd gotten killed back in Alaska."

"Don't they have, like uhh, two warnings already? One more and we'll be sent after them."

"Wait, really?" Seven's eyes lit up. "Where did you hear this?"

"Nine and I talk a lot." She replied.

Most operatives ratted each other out in order to be safe from the boss' watchful eye and vengeful spirit. A good salary was the glue that kept the organisation together. Operatives exchanged their freedom and safety for money.

"I could kill Zero and Three," Seven said. "I mean, I've got more experience. I was in the army before this shitty-ass job."

"I feel like any one of us could finish those two off. Zero is a fucking idiot who can barely use a gun and Three, well, he's also a fucking idiot."

"You're right," Seven said, loading his pistol magazine. "I feel bad about killing Four. He's a nice guy."

"He trained me a little before I became the new *One*. I think he also handled my predecessor, shot her in the head or something. By the way, what happened to the previous *Seven*? Anyone ever told you?"

"She fell off a building in an accident. Six said something about her being loyal, like really loyal to the boss, so I think someone shoved her down." Seven responded, staring at the passing streetlights as they drove.

"I would've shoved that bitch, too." One snorted, bringing the car to a halt as the traffic lights changed to red.

"Yeah, who wouldn't have?" He laughed. "I shoved the previous Two off a building. I still feel bad about that, the guy couldn't have been more than twenty-five."

"Wait, that was you?" One turned to face her partner.

"Yeah, it was," he mumbled. "Were you two close?"

"Fuck, no! He tried to get me terminated for mentioning that a vacation would be nice." She put the car in first gear and drove off as the light turned green.

"Oh, wow."

"So, thank you for your service."

"You're welcome, I guess."

Four's ex-wife's house was known by everyone in the organization. A sign that any operative could threaten his security whenever the boss wanted. The house had lights on, and the ex-wife, Jane Vasquez, was cooking in the kitchen. One spotted Four's car that was parked a few houses down. She gave Seven a look that said *let's get this bullshit over with* before stepping out of the vehicle and sneaking toward the peaceful home. Seven entered the backyard and One decided to test her luck by knocking on the front door. It didn't take long for her senior to open the door. He didn't look surprised, seeing her.

"I think you know why I'm here," she pulled her jacket to the side, revealing a handgun tucked into the waistband of her jeans. "You should tell Jane to–"

A loud scream, begging for help interrupted One's warning. She knew Seven had the frightened woman in his grasp. Four looked calm, yet she could feel his blood boiling. "I take it you brought someone with you?" He asked, and One nodded as she raised her weapon to point at him.

"Can we talk before you two do anything?" He inquired.

"Sure," One shrugged her shoulders. "Kitchen?"

Four entered the kitchen to see Jane, sobbing silently by the table as Seven held her at gunpoint. "I think you can leave her be, Seven." She said when Four sat across the table from his ex-wife. One's partner apologized as he holstered his weapon.

"So… What is it, Four? You know you have kick the bucket tonight."

"Are you fond of Evelyn?" Four asked the two operatives.

"*Hell no.*" Both answered, simultaneously.

"Yet, you still choose to carry out his vicious commands?" He asked, alternating between the pair. "Did he take every last bit of your humanity as you shook hands?"

"He didn't." Seven replied, but Four didn't look convinced.

"You, Seven, broke into her house and held her at gunpoint just to get to me. She had the decency to at least knock on the door to get to me."

"Now that you say it like that, Seven, that was kind of an asshole move." One glanced at her partner who looked *guilty*. "You're right," he turned to look at Jane. "I'm sorry, really."

Jane glared at the man who had held her hostage. Seven had done worse things during the four years he had worked for Evelyn. "You've worked for this damn organisation for what? Fifteen years?" One ran her fingers through her hair. "You must've seen many attempts at rebelling. They never work, another operative always ends up dead. I've killed my colleagues to ensure my safety, knowing that any moment someone could return the favor."

"Everyone needs to turn against Evelyn." Four responded, as if it was the easiest thing in the world.

"How can that work?" Seven asked. "You know how some of us are."

"Zero and Three, I feel like they would turn anyone in now that they're on thin ice." One said, and her partner hummed in agreement.

"Oh, yeah," Four realized. "Fuck those two, then."

"Do you plan on just getting everyone to jump Evelyn?"

"Yes," their senior nodded. "I sure would love to jump him. The bastard didn't let me retire in peace and sent some dumbasses after me."

"Yeah, that was... Fucked up." Seven mumbled, avoiding Jane's glare.

"Are you on board? Can I trust you *won't* kill me?" Four asked the pair. One nodded while Seven hesitated for a moment before agreeing. The kitchen fell silent as the operatives waited for their senior to explain what he knew of their shared employer, but that moment never came.

A red dot appeared on the pair's chests. It settled right on top of their hearts. Four looked defeated, yet relieved. He used the oldest trick in the book, trust. Seven turned to face his partner, and One did the same. They knew what was coming next: a bullet straight to the chest.

"Thirty-one," she said. "My birthday is on the thirty-first, that's why I'm *One*."

"Seventeen, well, Seven." He smiled.

ESCAPE ARTIST

"Is that you, *Victoria?*" Oh, God. I knew that high-pitched voice. It was Dana, someone I went to high school with almost two decades ago. We had English and math together, and we were both in the student council. "Yes, Dana, it's me. What are you doing here?" I thought moving to another country would've helped me avoid some of these assholes from my past, at least.

"I heard Stockholm was trendy but not too trendy, and wanted to avoid the big crowds," Dana adjusted her jacket. "What about you, Victoria? How did you end up in Sweden? Where do you live, still back at home?" Ah, yes, I had forgotten how her questions hid insults. I shook my head and responded: "I live here. What about you, do you still live there?" I could see the surprise she tried to hide.

"In a bigger city, but close to home." I smiled, smugly at her. It made my day better, knowing Dana hadn't moved too far in her life. "Good for you, Dana," I said. "Well, I need to get going."

"Since you live here, why don't we get coffee this week? I'm leaving next Wednesday." I stopped to think about it. I'm curious; I want to know if she has a shitty job, a spouse who's unfaithful, or children who refuse to speak to her.

"Sure, are you free tomorrow?" She nodded. We agreed to meet at a café near her hotel. Coffee with Dana was a risk in my books, but I was too curious.

The next day, I was there, waiting for Dana. She arrived late, sat down without apologizing, and started bombarding me with questions. *Do you have a boyfriend? What do you do for work? Why did you move to Sweden? Where did you go to university? How are your parents?* It felt like I was being interrogated by her, a high school acquaintance, who I basically hated. I noticed the ring on her finger, pointed at it, and asked who she was married to, hoping it wasn't a happy marriage. "Theodore, you remember him, right?" Of course, I remember him. The guy was a nuisance. No wonder, these two got married. It didn't take long for Dana to get back on the topic of my love-life.

When Dana left to go use the bathroom, I felt I had had my fun. I left without an explanation and blocked her number, hoping to never bump into her again. Two years later, I'd see her again in Rome. I sat near the Colosseum, looking at the ancient monument when she tapped me on the shoulder. Dana didn't look angry about our last encounter or maybe she was, I'll never know because I said hello and disappeared into a crowd of tourists, leaving Dana and her husband where I had sat for some time.

DON'T LIMIT YOURSELF

A powerful hit collided to the side of my head. I felt my skull exploding into a million pieces, and I fell to the floor. The invincible force, destroying my brain, left no traces of its existence. My eyes stayed open, staring at the popcorn ceiling stained with gore. It wasn't red, it was every shade under the sun.

The floor wasn't hard; my unmoving corpse sunk through it. My floor and my downstairs neighbor's ceiling became the in-between. It was an omnipresent space. My brain had exploded everywhere, I was no longer constricted. Freedom tasted sweet, like eating birthday cake or candy. I felt my smashed teeth tingle, wondering if a cavity would form because I tasted liberty.

The in-between felt like an eternity, but I fell through in seconds. I ended up back on my own floor, falling fast on the hard surface. Pain shot through my body, but I felt my head was in one piece again.

PURIFICATION HALTED

Gin tonics, white wine and vodka sodas, maybe even overpriced bottled water. The occasional turbulence had spilled drinks here and there, and the pair had to beg for more napkins from the flight attendants. Mariana rested her head against the window, looking at the city lights of Central Europe. She had lost track of what country they were flying over after the third drink. For a moment, fog filled her brain, and she struggled to remember their destination. Her doctor advised to drink less. *It'll help you in the long run*, the expert said after her last visit to the rheumatologist.

"What are you thinking about?" Her friend, Aloisio, asked.

"The fucking rheumatologist," she sighed. "And her advice."

"What did the doctor tell you?" He poured the rest of the white wine in her empty plastic cup.

"To drink less," she snorted before chugging the cheap liquid. It tasted like hand soap mixed with honey, but she still swallowed it all without complaints. She took what she could.

"*Oh*," he stared at her. "You've followed her advice well."

"I   just   don't   see   her   point."

"Why's that?" She noticed the strange look in his eyes. Mariana tried to figure out what *that* look was. The doctor had pitied her but not him. He just wanted her to spill the beans and get it over with, so they could move on to another topic.

"Well, can I not get shit-faced and forget for a little while that my goddamn tissue is hardening?" She explained.

"Makes sense." He replied, taking a drink from his cup. Aloisio approached her anxiety like some sort of therapist; he didn't feed into her negative thoughts. She wanted him to ask more, get her going to the point she might cry.

"Why does it make sense?" She inquired. "I mean, the professionals know it'll make it worse."

"Temporary relief." He responded as if it was obvious. The doctor, her mother and friends argued with Mariana about choosing healthier coping strategies. He just agreed with her.

"You're not as aware of the impending doom." She added and Aloisio nodded, humming in agreement.

"It's unfair," Mariana said, quietly. "I'd rather get a bone broken once a month than feel like the grim reaper's knocking on my door every day."

"In your case, has it always been because of something you can't control?"

"Yeah," she sighed. "How about you?" She asked.

"I'm certain I'll be the reason. Accidental or not, I don't know yet."

"If it were accidental, then it'd be something you couldn't control." She said, confused.

"I might drink myself to death by accident." He laughed. Mariana thought about it, an image of him popped into her head, and she snickered.

"I'm jealous," she giggled, somber. "I'd rather be the reason for my demise. All me and nothing else."

"Wouldn't it be funny if we could switch?" He proposed, and Mariana nodded without hesitation. She knew it wasn't possible, yet the idea entertained her. If only the universe allowed it.

"Want to get more drinks?" Aloisio asked when he spotted one flight attendant, walking down the rows of seats. "Unless you want to listen to your doctor's advice?" He added. She pondered for a moment: "If you're paying," she started. "Get me another gin and tonic."

"Sure, I'll pay. Anything else? You should at least eat something, or you'll have a worse hangover."

"Chips?" She said. Aloisio was right; if she kept up her drinking, soon she'd be hunched over a toilet, wishing she'd stopped at three.

"Want to bet when they're going to cut us off?" Mariana proposed.

"You owe me twenty if they stop serving us after, uhm, two more rounds." Aloisio replied.

"Then, you owe me twenty if they stop after three more." She said. The pair shook hands, sealing their stupid bet. "What do we do if they refuse to give us more after this? Or wait, refuse to serve now?" He asked, genuinely worried.

"I didn't think about that," she laughed. "Act sober, so we can get more."

"I'm basically clear-headed unlike you." She frowned at his statement.

"Move over, I'm going to the bathroom otherwise I'm going to fuck this up. Move over, damn." Mariana said. She managed to leave her row, leaving Aloisio to deal with the flight attendant. She hadn't moved during the whole flight, and felt like a new-born deer, learning how to walk. The plane went up and down as she tried to keep herself standing. Her mind was coherent, but the rest of her body was slowly succumbing to the effects of alcohol. The pathway to the end of the plane slid from side to side, like a snake coming toward her. She gripped the seats, giving herself the balance to move forward.

Mariana jumped inside the bathroom and locked the door with numb hands. She slumped against the weak wall. It felt like gravity was trying to pull her through the floor and make her meet the ground thousands of meters below. The woman in the mirror looked unrecognizable; she looked older, sadder, and sicker. Dark eyebags, pale skin, and empty eyes. Mariana had only turned twenty-three, yet she felt fifty-three. An age she knew she probably won't see. She looked down at her hands to see them turning blue—

Knocking gained her focus back to the present. She fumbled with the lock before managing to open the door. Another passenger, an older woman with hauntingly similar facial features to hers, stood there. "Other people need to use the bathrooms, young lady." The woman said, rudely.

"Ma'am–" Mariana started.

"Twenty minutes, girl." The passenger cut her off. The woman's voice sounded muffled to her ears. Inside the bathroom, time had stopped for Mariana, and she had forgotten about everyone else.

"I'm sorry," she slightly slurred her words. "The lock was complicated." The old woman looked horrified, hearing her voice. Quickly, she returned to her row, trying hard to seem sober. She looked over her shoulder to see the older passenger converse with one flight attendant who kept his gaze fixed on her.

"Jesus Christ, I thought you had passed out–" Aloisio said when he noticed her, gripping the aisle seat with white knuckles. "Goddammit, Mariana."

"Are you good?" He asked, helping her to the window seat.

"I– I guess, I mean, probably." She said.

"I'm glad the flight attendants refused to serve us." Aloisio gave Mariana the bag of chips he'd gotten for her.

"Neither of us won?" She asked. "What the fuck do we do now?"

"Let's worry about that later." He poured a cup of water for her.

"Were you not acting sober enough?"

"Me?" He laughed. "We saw you stumbling to the bathroom. You should've seen yourself, Jesus Christ."

"Fuuuuuck," Mariana threw her head back. "One more gin and tonic would've been amazing."

"It won't be long until we land, and you can get one." She felt her throat tighten in frustration. If she still were a toddler, she'd throw a fit, scream and cry and roll down the aisle in the sky.

"How long until we land?" She mumbled.

"What?"

"How long?" She raised her voice. "How long until we land?"

"Forty minutes, I think."

Mariana groaned and slumped in her seat, looking up at the buttons and air-conditioning. Desperation and anxiety started to build up, and the loud noises of the airplane made her claustrophobic. She saw the emergency exit door peak through the gap between the seat in front of her and the interior wall of the plane. Her right hand that rested on her thigh tried crawling toward it, but Mariana took hold of it with the remaining hand under her jurisdiction.

"How can you be so calm?" Mariana asked.

"I'm not." He replied.

"Does anything help? Man, I'm really fucking desperate."

"We just have to live with it."

"That's depressing," she responded. "Has your resistance already been worn down?"

"I never had much to begin with. It's not a hard task to tire me out." He concluded, smiling.

"I've noticed," she said. "Fight a little, you goddamn loser."

"I JUST WORK HERE"

This has to be some sick joke, Magdalena thought to herself. A rainy night, an empty bus stop, and an empty bus–her bus, drove toward her. She knew how it goes: wave down the bus, step inside it, and let it drive her around aimlessly. The bus came to a stop with the door directly in front of her, it opened, and she boarded the vehicle. No machine to show her pass and the cat who drove the bus didn't spare her a glance. *Just like last night.*

"Evening, Mr. Cat-driver or whatever you are." Magdalena muttered, walking to the back of the bus. She sat down on the old and worn-out seats.

"Do cats really have nine lives or is that just bullshit?" She yelled at the driver, hoping for some kind of acknowledgement. Every night, she asked a different question. Yesterday, she inquired if Mr. Cat had a high school diploma, and a few nights ago she asked if the cat had a favorite philosopher.

"Is it a stereotype that all cats hate dogs?" Magdalena got up from her seat and walked toward the driver. She was ignored, like always. She felt invisible, yet everything was done for her, as if someone knew what was best for her.

"Y'know, Mr. Cat, you not talking to me is kind of an asshole move," she said. "We've done this for as long as I can remember. *Every. Single. Night.*" Mr. Cat had basically watched Magdalena grow up, yet the cat had never paid attention to her as if the Mr. Cat was some emotionally absent father.

"At this point, I see you more than my own family." She sighed and returned to her seat, defeated once again. The raindrops fell with more force, overcoming the uncomfortable silence.

"Mr. Cat, I'm sorry for insinuating that you're an asshole," she apologized. "I'm just tired and confused, but I know it's not an excuse to say hurtful things." She had never before shown remorse toward the driver. She had used every colorful word to try to break down Mr. Cat's defenses, and Magdalena never succeeded. She thought changing her attitude would confuse the driver, and maybe she would get something out of the animal. However, it didn't work.

"What does all of this mean? I try to look for clues in my life: my friends, my family, my education, my past, my job, my future, my identity, my problems, Jesus Christ, everything! What does it mean to travel by bus and have a cat as a driver!" She screamed. Magdalena had thought about the possibility of Mr. Cat having ill intentions, but her gut never suspected a thing.

The bus came to a halt, an unexpected stop. Mr. Cat opened the door, and stepped out of the bus, standing on two feet. Magdalena followed the driver outside and noticed the cat had pulled out a box of cigarettes.

"I didn't know cats could smoke," she said. "A funny sight, I must admit."

"Look, I just work here." Magdalena stared at the cat, amazed that the animal finally answered her after over a decade. "Did *you* know that this– this has been torture. Horrendous psychological torture. Why? *Help me* understand, Mr. Cat."

"The medication could stop this." Mr. Cat said.

"What medication?" Magdalena asked.

"The one your psychiatrist described, and I'm not talking about the short-term one."

"I can't take it," she responded, smacking the cigarette carton from the feline's paws. "You take the goddamn meds."

"Why not?" Mr. Cat inquired. "It would help you. No more paranoia, obsession, or anger."

"What's left without it?"

"You'll be you. It won't change you, well, only remove the horrible parts. So, only the good will stay." Mr. Cat said.

"It keeps me together," Magdalena argued. "You don't know what you're talking about. You're a cat, a smoking cat. I don't take suggestions from chain smokers."

"You don't want to get better?" Mr. Cat asked.

"I do, of course I fucking do!"

"You won't lose yourself," the cat replied. "It's meant to help you, not shatter your sense of self. Do you really think that those negative things make you yourself?"

"It makes me, *me!* The paranoia and obsession and anger, yes, they're ugly, but how can I get myself out of bed in the morning if I'm not obsessed? How can I keep myself safe if I'm not paranoid? How can I hold my ground if I'm not angry? I have to be like this in order to push through."

"I think you're confusing obsession with passion, Magdalena."

"I think *you're* confusing obsession with passion, dumbass."

"Magdalena, you need to calm down." Mr. Cat demanded.

"Who are you to tell me that?" She asked, furious. "You don't have the right and neither does that psychiatrist."

"You do know that I'm a piece of you? I'm in your head, so *I do have the right*."

"You're a cat driving a bus! Why is there a cat bus-driver inside my head?"

"We really thought this was the night you'd understand," Mr. Cat said. "We're out of time today. I'll see you tomorrow."

Magdalena tried to argue with the damn cat, but with a snap of his strangely human-like paws—hands? Mr. Cat made everything go black. Soon, she woke up in a cold sweat, confused and scared. She sat up in her comfortable bed, looking around the room. She assumed the bad nights were back and an old topic had to be brought up to the shrink for the expert to poke around her brain.

MERRY EARLY CHRISTMAS

November 15th, 2039

The research institute was shaken by rough waves. The Pacific Ocean could be gentle or rough, and it was hard to predict. For some unknown reason, Evie, the nurse, had wandered outside. The whole crew felt the gigantic wave, hitting the floating vessel. Abigail's screams told everyone what they needed to know: Evie had gone overboard. The young woman couldn't be saved; she was now a part of the ocean. The first one to get to Abigail was Dex. He tried consoling her, but nothing could help her. After all, she just witnessed her friend being swallowed by violent waters.

"What happened?" Alexander, the other nurse, asked. Behind him, Nala and Seolhee tried to keep standing with the swaying vessel.

"Evie," Dex sighed. "She's gone."

"What do you mean she's *gone?*" Nala inquired.

"He means she's dead, Nala. Gone overboard." Seolhee clarified, coldly.

Abigail sobbed, trying to explain what had happened, yet she was unable to do so. Seolhee stared as the researcher tried to form words. All she could manage was *Evie* and *needing help.* "We can't help her," Seolhee mumbled. "We'll all lose our lives if we try." She decided to break the bad news to Abigail who wouldn't accept reality, and Abigail gave her the nastiest glare.

"We could radio for help?" Nala proposed.

"Isn't the radio still broken?" Alexander asked.

"We haven't managed to fix it yet," Dex placed his hand on the wall to steady himself as another wave shook the vessel. "The last set of waves caused a lot of damage."

"If we had better tools, maybe it could've been fixed already." Seolhee added.

"So, still no one knows we're stuck in the middle of the world's biggest ocean?" Nala asked, fighting back tears.

"Well, they'll figure it out by Christmas." Alexander responded. The floating research institute was set to return to the coast of Chile on the 22nd of December. The vessel set sail in early June, and the researchers and crewmen had been stuck since late October.

"We can continue fixing it, but we'd have to wait until the storm calms down. Otherwise, it's just dangerous with all the open wiring." Seolhee said. Out of the crewmen, who were there to ensure the vessel functioned properly, Johannes was the only one who knew the wiring best.

Another rough wave hit the vessel, the heavy water momentarily tried sinking it, but it jumped right back up, throwing the trapped souls around. Everyone ended on the floor, screaming, and trying to grab onto anything to hold themselves up.

November 19th, 2039

The lowest level of the floating research institute had a strange hole, dropping deeper into the depths. Inside it, there was crucial wiring that had been damaged. Johannes, the oldest and most experienced one, climbed down the steel ladder. "After this is fixed, we should try to work on the door." Everyone hummed in agreement. The door that needed fixing was damaged at the same time as the wiring of the radio. The broken door led to the storage room where all the lifeboats were.

"I think this fucking vessel was built to cause accidents," Noah stated. "I mean, this thing was supposed to withstand everything, and it hasn't."

"We should demand money for suffering." Seolhee added.

"That's a great idea!" Noah laughed.

"I doubt the university will pay us extra." Johannes said.

"Let's sue them. Originally ten of us and nine returned." Dex proposed.

"I'm down," Seolhee threw a flashlight to Johannes. "This thing is a faulty product. Did they even test-drive this before putting people on this vessel *and* sending it in the middle of the Pacific for what, six months?"

"What are the researchers supposed to *research* here?" Dex asked, curious.

"I don't know?" Noah shrugged. "They never talk about it. I asked Wynn and he said they have an NDA."

"That's wild." Seolhee said, bewildered.

"Johannes, did you know about the NDA?" Noah yelled, waiting for a response from the man down the hole. "Jesus, is he ignoring me? How loyal do you have to be to your employer?" Noah mumbled under his breath, loud enough that Dex and Seolhee heard him. They giggled, weakly. "Johannes?" He yelled, and once again no response. Noah walked to the edge of the hole. The sight waiting for him left him paralyzed with shock. Somehow, water had invaded the hole, and the open electrical wiring had ended the poor man. He lay there in an awkward position with his eyes and mouth open, screaming silently in agony.

November 21st, 2039

The remaining eight sat in the dining area. An overbearing silence that was now and then broken by Nala's weak sobbing. She and Johannes had been married for four years. Abigail tried holding her hand, but she pulled away from her touch. Noah and Dex had to seal the lowest room off. One of their two options was now gone. The water and open wiring made the hole a death trap, and no one could fix it unless Johannes would resurrect, and get to work.

"Is there another way to fix the radio?" Wynn asked, desperate.

"No," Dex buried his head in his hands.

"I need to be alone." Nala sobbed, running off to her and Johannes' room. Abigail followed her despite her pleas. The researcher knew she couldn't be left alone. The death of her husband, isolation at sea, and the death of Evie were a burden on her fragile mental state.

"How do we get help?" Carmen, one of the four researchers, asked.

"This is a long shot, but if we can get the storage room door fixed and open, a sturdy lifeboat might be our only option. It's honestly not a good idea." Noah said.

"We've already lost two people; we can't send anyone out in the Pacific on a lifeboat without any communication." Alexander replied.

"Yeah, I know," Noah sighed. "But I can't think of anything else."

"How much food do we have? Can we make it until Christmas?" Carmen inquired.

"If we ration really well, we should be fine until New Years." Seolhee responded, avoiding eye contact with the rest.

"Seolhee," Carmen started. "Are you saying that we could be stuck in the middle of nowhere for longer and maybe even die?"

"God, I hope not, but– forget it, I really don't know."

"Let's not talk about dying, okay?" Alexander demanded.

November 22nd, 2039

At night, Nala downed a bottle of pills. Abigail found her in the early hours of the morning. She alerted Alexander, the only remaining person with medical knowledge on the vessel, but it was too late. She had died most likely hours ago, and she could no longer be saved. Nala didn't leave a note, and she didn't need to.

"Just fix the damn storage room door!" Abigail yelled, crying.

"We don't have the right tools," Seolhee tried showing her the most useless toolbox she had seen during her career. "We need the right ones to not damage it further!"

"You, Dex, and Noah are supposed to be one of the best, and you can't even improvise?" Abigail retorted, harshly.

"There's nothing we can use–" Noah tried explaining, but the panicking researcher interrupted him: "Oh, God! Why did they pick you useless pieces of shit!"

"Abigail, please, calm down." Carmen intervened, placing her hand on her colleague's shoulder. Abigail roughly pushed her hand away. "How are you this calm? Three people are dead!"

"We need to stay calm. There's nothing else we can do!" Carmen raised her voice.

"Does the research laboratory have anything we could maybe use?" Seolhee asked as Abigail was escorted into the dining area by Wynn and Alexander. Carmen sighed, shrugging her shoulders: "I can't really say since I don't know what you need. It's against protocol to let you inside the laboratory–"

"Fuck the protocol, we have three dead, and our radio is impossible to fix." Noah groaned.

"I really don't know," Carmen hesitated. "There has to be a reason why it's strictly off limits." Truthfully, the researcher didn't care about protocol, but she was worried for her career. Breaking the rules wouldn't be looked upon lightly in her field.

November 26th, 2039

The researchers refused to let Seolhee, Dex, and Noah enter the laboratory. Abigail kept insisting as professionals they'd figure something else out. Noah had gotten more heated as each day was passing, and Alexander had to step in to calm the situation down, but the nurse had been unsuccessful.

"Seolhee said we have enough food to pull through until we're rescued," Carmen stood before the entry of the research laboratory. "The lifeboats are also not a good idea."

"You all keep bitching about us needing to figure something out and when there's a possibility you don't want us to take it?" Noah inquired, almost yelling.

"Don't talk to us that way—" Abigail screamed.

"Everyone, we need to stay calm!" Alexander stepped in between Noah and Abigail. Dex and Seolhee knew Noah better than the rest; he was a jokester, but the man could lose his temper easily. Noah was dangerously close to crossing a line, and they knew it.

"You should agree that this is bullshit!" Noah snarled at Alexander who motioned the researchers to leave them alone.

"I get your point, Noah, really I do," Alexander kept his arm extended to keep Noah away from him. "But think about it, the lifeboats don't have any radios and you'd just be floating in the ocean. There's no way of knowing if a boat or a plane sees you."

"I'd rather float in the fucking ocean than be inside this *thing* especially with these researcher people."

"Noah, it's better to stay here. You'll lose your shit alone." Seolhee said. Dex tried to grab his arm to guide him elsewhere, but Noah had other plans. He ripped his limb free and got into Alexander's face. He pushed the nurse backward.

"Stop it!" Dex tried to intervene, but Noah pushed him away. He shoved Alexander again. Seolhee and Dex tried to pull him away again, but his size and strength overpowered both. His final rough shove of the nurse pushed Alexander against a wall. The back of his head violently hit the pipes. The man crumbled before Noah, Dex, and Seolhee. A puddle of blood began to form on the floor, coating their messy shoes.

November 27th, 2039

Noah was locked inside his shared room with Dex. He didn't fight when Wynn, Dex, and Seolhee forced him inside. The death of Alexander was bad luck, but it could've been avoided if Noah kept calm. "Both of our nurses are dead! Who can help any of us now?" Abigail ranted, walking around the dining area.

"We just have to be extra careful." Wynn stated. Seolhee and Carmen hummed in agreement. Dex sat at the big white table in the middle of the area, covering his head in his hands. Noah and he had been good friends before they took the job of working on the research institute.

"Could you two not control your friend?" Abigail hissed, focusing on Seolhee.

"Have you seen the guy? We tried, we really tried." Seolhee replied, sharply.

"You didn't try hard enough." Abigail said. Seolhee stood up from her seat and walked up to the researcher. Wynn was there to stop her. "See? All of you are like Noah. No wonder, you worked so well together. We should be more worried about these two being here with *us*." Abigail continued.

"Can you shut the fuck up for one goddamn moment? All you do is complain and never do anything about this situation. What Noah did is unforgivable, but that doesn't mean me and Dex will pull the same shit. We want back on land, and you aren't helping." Seolhee responded from behind Wynn.

"Fuck you," Abigail huffed. "Fuck you, fuck you!" The researcher left the dining area. Seolhee wondered what Abigail's problem with her was. At the briefing, back in

April, she already knew they wouldn't get along. She saw Abigail as entitled, spoiled, and stubborn. Someone like her wasn't cut out to work in a team. Right now, they had to work as one if they wanted to avoid another death.

"What's her problem with me?" Seolhee asked, focusing on Carmen. The other researcher sighed and shook her head. She didn't know. Wynn didn't know either. Seolhee knew it would stay a mystery until the end of time.

"Can we please get inside the laboratory?" Dex whispered. Wynn and Carmen looked at each other before silently agreeing. The group made their way to the entry, ignoring the dried blood on the floor.

"We can't tell you what we're researching, okay?" Wynn said as the door opened.

"We really don't care." Seolhee replied. The laboratory had white walls, workstations, and more closed doors. Seolhee and Dex looked around for anything that could be used as a tool, but it was a useless search.

December 2nd, 2039

Noah had fallen ill. He started vomiting blood a few days ago. The remaining crew decided not to help him. His disease could kill the rest of them. Out of curiosity, Carmen watched the ill man through the security cameras. He writhed in pain. The room was destroyed and full of blood splatters. The man groaned, pleaded, and cried for help. Carmen, Wynn, and

Abigail had agreed to feed him once a day before he fell sick. They had not told Dex and Seolhee about their decision.

"Do you think he'll die?" Wynn asked, quietly from the entrance to the security room.

"I do," Carmen replied, shutting the screen off. "I doubt it'll take long." The researcher was right. Noah was dead when the sun began to set. He choked on his own bloody vomit.

Seolhee and Dex sat in the dining area, sharing a protein bar. They kept quiet, mourning the death of Noah even if his poor choices led to Alexander's end. The thought of jumping on a lifeboat and letting it take them wherever the ocean wanted, started sounding appealing to Dex.

"Let's try fixing the door." Dex proposed. Seolhee stayed quiet, knowing it was a stupid idea, but the isolation and dying colleagues bothered her.

"Sure," she replied. "Let's try to fix it."

The pair grabbed the useless toolbox and set out to fix the door. First, they tried with some hope. Then, they tried forcing it open. Lastly, they sat, leaning against the wall, hopeless. The door wouldn't budge.

December 6th, 2039

Dex started vomiting blood only a day ago. He died faster than Noah, and it was gruesome. Abigail, Carmen, and Wynn forced Seolhee inside the only room that wasn't occupied. The remaining researchers insisted she was contagious since she had spent time with Dex and Noah before they got sick. Dex hadn't mentioned any symptoms before he started throwing up. In a second, he was dying. The researchers hadn't spoken with her since locking her up. They only opened the door to give her food. Each of them held a pocketknife, pointing it at her, telling Seolhee to stay away as they dropped a protein bar or a water bottle for her. She didn't touch the food or liquid.

She walked to the door and banged on, hoping that one of the researchers was nearby. She wanted to know what they knew about the disease. They never mentioned anything about her friends' deaths. As Dex was dying, the researchers pointed a knife at her and forced Seolhee inside this room. The security room was supposed to be a haven, yet now it was her prison.

Her banging went unnoticed, or it was *ignored*. She wanted to think the best about the researchers, but they had ignored Noah and Dex, so she wasn't getting special treatment. Seolhee decided to continue with trying to crack the code to the security cameras. She was tired of being kept in the dark. She already tried the easy combinations. Seolhee knew only the researchers had access to the footage. Four numbers, that was all she needed to turn the screen on. She didn't know much about them, but she had a good memory. They celebrated Carmen's birthday before the vessel set sail, Wynn's, and Abigail's on board. *1005*, Carmen's didn't work. *2206*, Wynn's didn't work. *1307*, Abigail's didn't work. *5001*, backwards didn't work. *6022*, backwards didn't work. *7031*, bingo.

Seolhee giggled in victory. The screen lit up, revealing the sealed off lowest floor. The body of Johannes was still down the hole. The thought of his decaying corpse nauseated her. Seolhee saw Dex's lifeless body contorted in agony. Finally, she found the researchers inside the dining area. They sat around the big table. Wynn had his arms crossed, Abigail looked pissed, and Carmen was *just sad*. She pressed the button for audio to hear what they were talking about.

"What do we do about her?"

"We just have to wait for her to eat or drink what we've given her."

"Did we really have to do this to Dex and Seolhee?"

"Less mouths to feed. It's better for our survival."

"And they didn't deserve to survive, is that what you mean?"

"We have something to give to the world. We're important."

"After we're rescued, what do we tell everybody? They'll know there was no sickness. We're murderers."

"We dispose of the bodies."

"...Oh my God."

"It's our only choice. We are just protecting ourselves; this isn't murder."

"No, no, no. We're just– fuck, this is so messed up."

"Don't start falling apart now."

At night, Seolhee opened the protein bar, hid it, and left the wrapper on the security room's table. She emptied half of the water bottle in a corner and placed it near the wrapper. She lay on the floor with her back facing the entrance, waiting for one of the researchers to come check on her. Her only chance at survival was taking out these three playing God. She heard footsteps getting closer to the security room. Seolhee tried identifying them, hoping it'd be Abigail. A deep hatred of her had filled Seolhee's soul.

The door opened, and someone stepped inside the room. For a moment, the unknown person didn't move. Then, the researcher walked up to Seolhee and crouched down. A hand shook her body, but she stayed limp. Two hands took a hold of her bicep, as the person was pulling her on her back, Seolhee opened her eyes to see Carmen. She was disappointed but lunged anyway. She hit the researcher's nose, and a satisfying crack was heard. Carmen lost her balance and fell on her side. In the blink of an eye, Seolhee was on top of her, choking her. The researcher couldn't make any noise but tried to scratch and hit her attacker. Carmen was dead within minutes of encountering Seolhee, the colleague she'd locked in a room.

She searched Carmen's pockets, hoping to find the pocketknife. The weapon was in her right pocket. She gripped the knife in her right hand, tightly. Seolhee heard another set of footprints closing in on her. In the dark room, she hid behind a cabinet near the open door. It didn't take long for Wynn to appear, he froze in place, staring at the corpse. With hesitant steps, he walked closer to the dead woman. He lowered himself enough to touch her neck, feeling for a pulse, and then Seolhee stuck the knife deep in his neck, her goal was to inflict as much damage as she could.

December 11th, 2039

In the dining area, Abigail sat tied to a chair. Seolhee sat at the big table, eating a protein bar with another waiting for her. She didn't have to ration anymore since everyone was dead, and Abigail, well, she didn't deserve food. Seolhee felt slightly disgusted with herself for feeling the intense urge to make Abigail suffer, but she buried her shame without much difficulty.

"I'm thirsty." Abigail whispered. Seolhee had only given little water to her twice a day.

"Not yet," Seolhee took another bite of the protein bar. "In about two or three hours, you'll get your little drink."

"You evil bitch."

"You're the *evil bitch*."

"Are you going to starve me to death?" Abigail asked. Seolhee wondered for a moment and then nodded, and the researcher began sobbing violently, begging for forgiveness she wouldn't get during this lifetime.

Abigail looked like a skeleton. Her limbs had thinned, almost slipping out of her ropes, so Seolhee tightened them. The researcher could barely speak anymore, and the other felt she had had her fun. Seolhee lightly slapped the woman awake.

"Hi, Abigail," Seolhee waved a bottle of water in front of her face. "It's almost Christmas and I want to do something nice for you, so merry early Christmas."

Seolhee drank the water bottle and threw it on the floor. She used the pocketknife to cut her ropes and helped her up. Abigail's eyes lit up, hopeful Seolhee had a change of heart. She grabbed the researcher by the nape and guided her out of the dining area into the hallway.

The pair ended up on the deck. The sun was hidden behind clouds, and the ocean was getting restless. Seolhee forced Abigail closer to the rails. "Please, can I have something to eat?" The frail woman pleaded but the other one stayed quiet. Seolhee didn't give her time to resist before pushing her over the rails. The waves swallowed Abigail in seconds.

Seolhee returned inside the research institute, locking the door behind her just in case the bitch somehow survived and crawled back on the vessel. Inside the dining area, a disco ball had dropped down from the ceiling. Soon, music from the 80s started playing. A voice from the intercom yelled, happily:

Congratulations to the winner!

*Con   gratulati   ons   t   o   th   e   winn
            er!*

HINT OF LEMON

The burning house behind us was never a distraction. We never cared for it; she only asked me if I knew what the man on the phone said as firemen were called. Years later, the memory is distant, appearing in my head as I yearn for warmth, standing under heavy snowfall with my fingers turning blue. She gave me a can of sardines as I struggled to open the fork packet. The utensils weren't plastic, a detail that has been burned into my mind. We ate the sardines straight out of the container. The fish swam in a pool of olive oil. My tongue recognized the hint of lemon that had seeped into the meat. I still remember the taste; the flavors forever connected to constant sunshine, blue skies meeting the ocean, and someone who I doubt would recognize me if we somehow crossed paths.

PARASITE

Who doesn't love tattoos? They're beautiful pieces of art made specifically for your body. A fun way to express your personality, creativity, or style. A tattoo is on your skin forever, so it can be a tough commitment for some, but also a passion for others. Tattoos hurt your wallet, that's true, however, it doesn't matter; money comes back. If you want it, my advice is to just get it. Older generations might judge you, but fuck what others think about you. It's your body and you get to do whatever you want with it as long as you don't hurt anybody.

I got my first tattoo at seventeen, and it took a lot of begging from my parents. I could've waited, well, I should've waited, but the past can't be changed. At eighteen, my parents couldn't stop me from getting more. When my wallet became heavier, parts of my skin were filled with black ink. I had never been a fan of colorful and vibrant tattoos—don't get me wrong, they're cool, and I appreciate art in every form, but they aren't for me. Black ink just suits my personality and style better.

Over the years, my arms, chest, and legs got more covered. Some of my tattoos had meaning and some didn't. My latest piece was abstract like my first one. I fell in love with lines, whether it was bold, thin, or delicate, I couldn't tear my eyes off them. The healing process was a pain in the ass, I mean, it always was. I didn't mind it; if I took care of it like a newborn baby for four weeks, my chances of it lasting were better. My least favorite part of the healing process was the itching, it drove me insane every single time. This time something was different, worse. The itching was worse. For a moment, I wondered if it had gotten infected, but my skin wasn't red, just itchy.

After two weeks, I couldn't take it anymore. I scratched and scratched and scratched and scratched and scratched. I tried to avoid the tattoo itself but after the torturous itching I could care less. It never hurt, but as I scratched, the itching became more intense. I felt it spreading all over my body. *An allergic reaction or an infection after all?*

I stopped to inspect the area after aggressive scratching. My nails were painted red; I had broken skin. Cursing under my breath, I tried to wipe the blood away with a paper towel. Red and black mixed together. The bleeding became stronger, and stopping it was impossible. The liquid was far too dark, and panic began to settle in.

The blood turned black as midnight as if all the ink in my body was escaping to my wooden floor. To my horror, that was exactly what was happening. The rest of my tattoos faded before my eyes until I looked like my sixteen-year-old self, a bare canvas, waiting to be filled with art of my choosing.

The puddle of ink beneath my feet was huge, and my apartment smelled like the tattoo studio I frequented. I stepped away from the puddle, leaving behind footprints.

A bump formed in the middle of it. It grew and grew and grew and grew. A big *thing* stood before me, and it was getting even *bigger*, expanding slowly but surely. The thing was everything yet nothing at the same time, *a perfect abstraction*. My inner voice spoke like my high school art teacher.

I backed away from the growing ink being, but my back met the wall in seconds. The ink being reached my other wall before it did me, and I heard the crack. The damn thing was breaking my apartment with its huge size. Everything was covered by black, but I knew the thing hadn't reached me yet. I couldn't scream, and I just waited until it swallowed me.

As the black ink surrounded me, I lost all feeling. I became light, lighter than a feather. I could no longer feel my limbs or see anything. It felt like floating in space—*what I imagined floating in space felt like*; I'm not an astronaut. The lovely zero gravity feeling left as quickly as it came. I was *the dark space*, and something was pushing and pulling me, trying to mold me. Soon, an uncomfortable tightness overwhelmed me. *Paralyzing*, that was how it felt.

I tried to force myself to move, to shake off the tightness. With unlimited strength, I continued for some time—a long time, I didn't know, time felt like it had stopped, I didn't know, it felt like I was in *something*, what was happening I didn't know, it was scary and confusing, I wanted to—

Light bursted in the space, and the tightness was gone. Faster than a cheetah, I flowed everywhere. No longer in darkness, my vision was back. I saw a ceiling and felt something stepping on me. Soon, a familiar face stared down at me. *I* smiled at myself, eyes fully black, and leaking of dark liquid as my teeth were coated with it. The person over me touched me, and her hand was coated in black liquid. *Ink.* She licked her hand clean, coating *my* tongue with it, covering the pinkish muscle.

My vision split in two; staring up at *myself* and staring down at a *puddle.* It was nauseating, watching myself lick the floor clean of the black ink. As she—or me—licked, her finger clean, my vision was restored to one. *Tasty. Tasty. Tasty. Tasty. Tasty.* That word kept repeating in my mind, it wasn't me. It was the thing. I was stuck again; my limbs didn't move with *my* command. They moved with *its* command.

Everything's fictional. I swear.

Meow. Meow. Meow.

Meow. Meow.

I think that's a sound a cat makes.

Thanks for reading.